The Last Pope

EGRESSION

JOHN OSTER

ISBN: 1-4392-0660-0
ISBN-13: 9781439206607

Visit www.booksurge.com to order additional copies.

For my folks: Jack, who introduced me to science fiction, and Pat, who showed me the love of reading

THE LAST POPE

A young boy from Valpolicella spent a summer on his uncle's sheep farm in Lombardy. Up early every day, he looked forward to helping with the chores, having a special affinity for the young lambs that seemed to be everywhere in the barns and fields. Far up the Val Seriana, surrounded by majestic peaks, sweeping emerald pastures, and endless azure skies, the life of a shepherd seemed very fine indeed.

One uncommon gloomy day, his cousin caught his arm when chores were over, and he forgot the threatening overcast in an instant.

"Luigi, today we go to Clusone to see the queen!" Luigi wondered about the sly smile on his cousin's face but only shrugged and held out his hands. *What queen?*

After breakfast the boys set off on bicycles. Fair where his cousin was dark, Luigi's open face drank in every detail as they passed vineyards, olive groves, and fields full of white-fleeced sheep. They rode almost every day, but this was the first time they took the winding path from tiny Rovetta to the much larger town nearby. Pedaling furiously as they passed a procession of what could only be tourists, they headed toward what appeared to Luigi to be the inevitable *piazza*, nestled somewhere ahead among the looming, centuries-old buildings. Following the narrow street, the boys slowed to avoid uneven cobblestones that could send them flying over handlebars. Finally, the cathedral came into view around a curve. Dismounting, Luigi looked around curiously. *What queen?* he still wondered. Around the square he saw a few people on foot, and nearby a pair of teenage lovebirds prepared to leave on the boy's scooter. All else seemed quiet.

Then, looking up at the side of an ancient chapel, he finally understood as his cousin's giggles turned to laughter. Painted *dell'affresco*, a panorama of medieval royalty, clergy, merchants, and others were variously supplicating or being slain by skeletal demons. He noticed tiny details: arrows, scrollwork, jewels, eyes, fingers. Arms spread wide over all, the Queen of Death reigned supreme.

Somehow, the grinning skull and her subjects had survived centuries of neglect with only minimal restoration. The queen looked out at him as if to say, *Someday you will be mine*. The hollow-eyed death's-head burned, and he knew he would never forget it.

~

Half a world away, she woke up screaming. Again. Bathed in clammy sweat, she untangled herself from the damp, twisted sheets, shaking her head to clear the images that still terrified her after so many years. She massaged her temples as she staggered to the tiny bathroom. Fumbling for the switch, she turned on the light. Big mistake.

Looking back at her from the mirror was a haggard face whose drawn features bore an uncanny resemblance to the source of her nightmares—her mother. Disheveled brown hair framed bloodshot green eyes. Tall, she leaned over the sink thinking, *This will never do*, as she washed and brushed. She recited the mantra learned from her last therapist: "I'm eighteen years old, I have my entire life in front of me, and I live in exciting times. Mother is long gone and has no more power over me." Sure.

There would be no more sleep this night.

It happened the way so many things do, in a moment of thoughtless routine—in the battered Ford, mother driving, toddler in a car seat behind her. At three, Carolyn had already realized, in the resigned manner of young children everywhere, that her life was dictated by the whims of her custodians. This morning was no different. Mother had wanted to see some friends, and the inconvenient daughter would simply have to ride along. Now they were headed home. Mother was smoking furiously while she drove, flicking ashes into the breeze and muttering about nothing in particular. Inhaling deeply from the stub, she tossed it out and rolled the window up.

Random convection drew the cigarette in through Carolyn's window, which Mother had cracked open in a minor concession to ventilation. The smoking butt landed on the tattered, yellow blanket covering the child's lower body where, as the little girl watched with incurious detachment, the material immediately began to smolder and then burst into flame. Unaware and preoccupied with her own imagined sorrows, Mother drove on.

Carolyn was finally discharged from the Cedars-Sinai Trauma Center eight months later. The middle-aged grandparents who picked her up said little to the doctors and nurses who stopped to bid the child farewell. They didn't have to. Thirty-five weeks of constant misery, multiple surgeries, and imperfect recovery had etched themselves on the girl's face. At the end, in a last, desperate effort to save her legs, the medical team had employed a new reconstructive therapy based on molecule-sized repair engines developed in Sweden. It had required that the three-year-old be placed in a sterile metal cocoon that left only her head exposed. She had screamed the entire three days.

Exactly one week after the fire that nearly took his daughter's life, Carolyn's distraught father had sat on the living room couch and drunk himself nearly stuporous. He'd stared briefly into the barrel of the .38 caliber Smith & Wesson before putting it in his mouth and pulling the trigger, thereby ending both a troubled marriage and an equally troubled career in law enforcement. The sound woke his wife, upstairs in her own stupor. She took one look at the mess on the living room wall and grabbed her keys, never to be seen in L.A. again.

Carolyn's memories of her parents were quickly overlaid by the nightmare of her treatment. By the time she was wheeled out through the discharge lobby and loaded into her grandparents' long, gray Lincoln, her only thought was that she would never again allow "nanobots" to get anywhere near her. Thoughts of Mother were few and very far between. At first, anyway.

1

Images of his sister came, unbidden. He recalled a long-ago family vacation, when their parents had taken them on a North American tour that ended in Toronto atop the CN Tower, then the tallest structure in the world. He'd been fifteen at the time, three years older than Marie. As they stepped onto the elevator that would carry them 1,465 feet straight up, she had been paralyzed by acrophobic fear. He'd put his arms around her, held her close, and helped her through it. He remembered the clean, citrus smell of her hair.

The thought that the ride had been breathtaking at fifteen miles an hour brought a smile to his lips. The "elevator" in which he now rode was traveling ten times faster and was, well, enormous by comparison. It was in fact more aptly thought of as a luxury hotel suite, with comfortable leather and wood furniture fronting private sleeping and comfort areas. He would live in it for a week as it climbed thousands of miles up the tether that connected the departure lounge just outside the Kenyan city of Kisumu with the GEO (geosynchronous earth orbiter) station far overhead.

Gazing out one of the ports at the hazy, turquoise curve of the Earth far below, he wondered what Marie would have made of this experience. She had not survived beyond early middle age, electing to cloister herself with the good Sisters of Perpetual Devotion and refusing all advanced medicine when the need arose. He still missed her.

"Holiness?" The diffident voice of Father Bertani broke into his thoughts and he turned to his young minder. He had to suppress a smile; he knew the diminutive priest's constant worried expression had become a source of some amusement amongst the younger members of the Curia. And the confines of their temporary home had to be driving the obsessive cleric nuts.

"Si, Alberto? What is on your mind?"

"Forgive me, Holiness, but we have been asked by the GEO stationmaster for your itinerary. We have six more days of transit, but I wondered if you wished to begin sharing any details at this time. You know that the officials and the press are most anxious for any information you might care to share."

"Of course," Pope John XXIV said with a sigh. The 271st pontiff was also the first pope to travel into space, and the tumult in the media had been considerable. Speculation about his agenda and his "true" motives had occupied the editors and pundits for weeks, yet he had refused to divulge anything other than a timetable. But with his departure now an accomplished fact, he knew that freedom was about to come to an end.

"Give them the outline we prepared on the plane. It contains enough detail to give them plenty to speculate about until we arrive in orbit. I'd like to avoid getting more specific until we are able to converse in person with our ferry pilot, and that won't happen until we get to GEO station."

"As you wish, Holy Father," said Bertani as he turned to consult with the transit staffer assigned to their needs.

Glancing toward the horizon before returning to his seat, the pope noted a large spiral in the clouds far below. After a moment, he realized from its counterclockwise spin and clear center that it must be an early season hurricane barreling across the Atlantic. Huge. Implacable. He offered a silent prayer for those in its path and made his way to his seat amid the group of Curia officials selected to accompany him on the trip. He was not anxious for conversation but knew it was unavoidable under the circumstances. His companions were along ostensibly for support, but nothing was ever quite what it seemed in the world's oldest bureaucracy.

> *SANTA FE, N.Mex. – With advances toward ultra-strong fibers, the concept of building an elevator 60,000 miles high to carry cargo into space is moving from the realm of science fiction to the fringes of reality.*
>
> *This month, the Los Alamos National Laboratory was a sponsor of a conference to ponder the concept.*
>
> *The discovery in 1991 of nanotubes, cylindrical molecules of carbon with*

> *many times the strength of steel, turned the idea from a fantastical impossibility to an intriguing possibility that could be realized in as little as a decade or two.*
> *NEW YORK TIMES*, SEPTEMBER 23, 2003

Of course, it had taken more than a decade or two, but a hundred years after the Los Alamos conference, over a dozen installations now routinely sent people and goods on a leisurely climb up out of the gravity well. Kisumu was among the most popular departure points, matched in volume only by Ecuador's Quito. There had been some spectacular failures in the early days, but the system had been operating flawlessly for decades—long enough to satisfy the Curia and the Swiss Guard anyway.

The pontiff took his seat. Across the aisle, Cardinal Josef Rauschman was engrossed in what appeared to be the drafting of a lengthy document. He glanced up at the pope and greeted him with a thin smile.

"Holy Father, do you find the view to be inspiring?"

"Just so, Eminence. It is the hand of God, and it is everywhere." The pope looked away, not wishing to show his repulsion for the man. At a youthful age, Rauschman had undergone extensive macroenhancement modifications. One eye had been replaced with an optical scanner, one ear with a digital audio extractor. He had also obtained a multiplex media interface on the side of his neck, giving him instant, direct access to any digital information. The enhanced Rauschman was indeed a formidable intellect, but was he any longer a human being? John XXIV was not sure. He admitted to himself that it might have been easier if the man had a less arctic personality. Rauschman's modifications were seemingly at odds with his reputation as an enforcer of orthodoxy, but the combination caused his adversaries great anxiety.

Closing his eyes, the pope leaned back and offered a brief prayer of repentance for his uncharitable thoughts. He then allowed his mind to drift to the days and weeks ahead and to the imperative that had compelled him to embark on this most unconventional papal journey.

~

Fifteen years earlier, Cardinal Luigi Amato had ascended the Throne of Peter, much to the surprise of just about everyone. A winemaker's son from the Valpolicella region of Veneto, he had spent a relatively quiet decade as cardinal of Venice. Unremarkable in appearance, inoffensive in behavior, he was beloved by his flock, ignored by the Curia. And that was the way he wanted it.

When the aging Pope Pius XIII had passed away, the ensuing conclave had dragged on for over a week with no consensus. The all-too-familiar divide between traditionalists and reformers appeared to harden with each successive ballot, and finally the Cardinal Camerlengo called a twenty-four-hour recess to enable the participants to meditate, pray, and hopefully come to their senses. He got more than he bargained for.

When the princes of the Church returned to conclave, the austere Cardinal Odinga of Kenya placed the name of Cardinal Luigi Amato into nomination. Forty minutes later, white smoke curled over the Vatican, and the world got to meet Pope John XXIV.

Traditionalists, including many in the Curia, were dismayed by the new pontiff's choice of name. Vatican II was still recent history to them, and they feared that the quiet man from Venice was signaling his intention to follow a path similar to his namesake's. His initial years in the Vatican were undistinguished, however, and they began to relax. He proved adept at keeping his own counsel while ensuring that the necessities were attended. Plans, oh yes, he had many—until the Hand of God touched him directly.

He remembered the day his personal physician, Dr. Lorenzo Crosetti, came to him with the news he had feared—that persistent aching in his joints was a symptom of midstage bone cancer. And he remembered the choice he'd made.

> *Once nanomachines are available, the ultimate dream of every healer, medicine man, and physician throughout recorded history will, at last, become a reality. Programmable and controllable micro scale robots comprised of nanoscale parts fabricated to nanometer precision will*

allow medical doctors to execute curative and reconstructive procedures in the human body at the cellular and molecular levels. Nanomedical physicians of the early 21st century will still make good use of the body's natural healing powers and homeostatic mechanisms, because, all else equal, those interventions are best that intervene least. But the ability to direct events in a controlled fashion at the cellular level is the key that will unlock the indefinite extension of human health and the expansion of human abilities.

COPYRIGHT 1998-2006, ROBERT J. FREITAS, JR., FORESIGHT NANOTECH INSTITUTE

By the middle of the twenty-first century, medical nanotechnology had become so well established as to be routine for catastrophic conditions. For those who could afford it, such treatment could in theory extend life indefinitely since microscopic nanobots could be programmed to carry out virtually any biological repair job. The Church had struggled for decades to evolve a consistent view of the technology, caught up in the apparent clash between the value of human life and the evil of unchecked technology. No encyclical ever made it past the draft stage.

John XXIV's passion, which drove him every day of his life, was to make the Church relevant to society, especially to the young. He had seen firsthand the ease with which successive generations cast it aside as they became infatuated with the technological marvels of the age. He knew the importance of the Church's teachings, and he knew that nothing had come along to replace the set of values so intrinsic to civilized behavior. He feared the future, for to him it looked not only godless but chaotic and self-destructive.

So Dr. Crosetti's grim news hit him on multiple levels. Death was not a pleasant prospect, but the end of civilization could not be tolerated. He had no choice. He secretly checked in to a Swiss clinic; only Crosetti and Father Bertani knew of his plans. He underwent two weeks of therapy as billions of specialized nano-sized robots coursed through his bloodstream, making the necessary corrections and excising all traces of the cancer. The procedure called for unusually careful management by the medical staff, since it would never do for the seventy-five-year-old pontiff to return to his flock completely rejuvenated and youthful in appearance. The nanobots were given very specific, very limited instructions.

He returned to the Vatican looking like what he was, a thin, ordinary, middle-aged man for whom regular exercise fell into the wishful thinking department. In good health for the first time in years, he seldom slept well; his mind would not stop turning his choices over and over, and he prayed every day that he had made the right one. He renewed his vow each morning to carry on, sometimes with shadows under his eyes. Now it seemed the time had come to begin in earnest.

2

A potato, twice the size of Manhattan.

Carolyn found herself unable to stop thinking of her about-to-be new home as anything else. She had seen the photography, read the background, even researched the early work on Eros all the way back to the historic Near-Shoemaker mission in 2001. She had also perused all the details on the subsurface boomerville community. And she had yet to get her mind around the fact that she had actually made the trip and was about to take up residence in asteroid #433, known to most as Eros.

In the crowded passenger lounge of the ferry, perhaps two dozen other travelers variously chatted, gazed out the ports, or watched the slow approach of their new home on the flat panel displays. The months-long journey was nearly over. As she looked around, Carolyn realized that she might well be the oldest person on the flight. Her companions had the open-faced, excited demeanor of true youth. Some featured obvious enhancements, but most simply had that Look.

No matter. Unwilling to leave the mother planet's warm embrace, she had delayed this journey for decades until her friends and family were all gone, either moved away, uploaded, or dead. Finally, she had no more reason to stay...and there had been many reasons to leave for a very long time.

> *WASHINGTON, D.C. – Speaking from the Capitol steps, Speaker of the House Angel DelToro made an impassioned plea for calm before a crowd estimated by police at over 400,000 and by event coordinators at over 1,000,000. Virtually all marchers were "Gen-Xers" and their children. Their leaders had spoken throughout the day about "economic imperialism" and "intergenerational war," denouncing the baby boom generation and its iron grip on the nation's resources and leadership.*
>
> *Speaker DelToro, himself a boomer, was forced to leave the dais as heckling turned nasty, then ugly. Talking later with reporters, he admitted fear for the country's future.*
>
> *Washington Post, June 28, 2024*

It could have been predicted; in fact, in some respects it was, but the monumental divide that sundered America's body politic in the twenties was probably unavoidable. Consider: between 1946 and 1964, over seventy-six million children were born in the United States. They grew up knowing the least deprivation, with the best nutrition, health care, and education of any group in history. They matured in a time of unprecedented economic growth. By 2020, their combined spending power was over $10 trillion. And by 2020, there were still over seventy million of them wandering around. Owning property. Drawing on society's entitlements, especially Social Security and Medicare. Controlling the engines of commerce. Electing politicians who made sure their privileged status was protected (only 21 percent of the population, but they ALL voted).

Meanwhile children and grandchildren, ready to take their turns, discovered that unlike their own parents, the boomers were unwilling to go gently into the night. By the third decade of the twenty-first century, bio- and nanotechnology were offering the promise of vastly extended, healthy lives, especially to those who had the means to afford the still-new, expensive procedures. Family assets that previously had passed from generation to generation were redirected into exotic health care for the elderly. In fact, "elderly" in many cases became an outdated word as the fifty-, sixty-, and seventy-year-olds began to look and act years younger.

These people just would not go away.

The resultant scarcity and overpopulation meant that violence was, of course, inevitable. It first manifested in the early twenties as isolated vandalism and beatings but quickly escalated; gated communities in suburban Maryland and the Virginia countryside were attacked by organized mercenaries who allowed the residents to flee, then destroyed everything in sight. A similar attack in the Napa Valley turned deadly when two homeowners used bootlegged rocket-propelled grenades to destroy the mercenaries' lead vehicle, prompting the attackers to skip the resident-removal step. One hundred homes and over two hundred lives were obliterated. Martial law followed, though those responsible were never identified.

After the marches and demonstrations of 2024, leaders called for a national meeting to examine and try to solve the dilemma. Although no one could have known it at the time, the Seattle Summit of 2025 marked a turning point in human history. For the first time, there was a public acknowledgement that the Earth was too small and that resources were required to make the solar system accessible to humanity. There was perhaps a less public acknowledgement that the needed steps would provide an escape valve for the forces threatening to dismember society.

The Seattle sessions had a decidedly international theme as well, since the boomer problem was not limited to the United States. One of the more visionary attendees was the president of Ecuador, who, after meeting with NASA officials and with several Seattle-area business leaders, announced his intention to construct the world's first space elevator. Similar announcements followed in Kenya, Indonesia, and Brazil, all countries with equatorial locations suitable for connection with orbiting geosynchronous platforms. An international investment consortium agreed to back the ventures.

Within five years, the first elevators were hauling cargo into space at a fraction of the cost of rocket-based systems. In 2033, the first passenger services began in Quito and Kisumu. Not surprisingly, most of the passengers were boomers, since they had the means to afford the trips and, not coincidentally, owned the transit services. Before long, Marriott, Hilton, Hyatt, and other resort chains began to fill up geosynchronous space.

Meanwhile the investment consortium, which included a number of forward-thinking business leaders, undertook a parallel venture while the elevators were under construction. Working from a mining and manufacturing base on the Moon, it began to assemble prototypical space ferries that were designed to use plasma-based propulsion systems. These designs had been around and tested for several decades; however, there were other major obstacles to overcome. For example, if one were to embark on a months-long sojourn through the inner solar system, one would need air, water, food, and enough elbow room and diversion to maintain one's sanity. Or one would need to sleep for a very long time.

Many animals hibernate, although mice have never been among them. But big changes may be ahead in the mouse world. Researchers have succeeded in putting mice, without harming them, into a state of suspended animation that looks suspiciously like that of a hibernating bear.

Dr. Roth said that no one yet knows if the procedure would work in humans, or even in higher mammals, and that finding out would require considerable research and testing. But he expects that within five years, humans could begin to benefit from the work.

New York Times, April 26, 2005

By the twenties, suspended animation had been in use for over a decade to assist in the treatment of severe medical conditions, and it was a relatively simple task to migrate the existing technology to a deep space use. Consortium scientists combined the medical procedure with specially designed nanobots that performed complementary maintenance functions while their human hosts dreamed away. One problem solved.

Scientists funded by the European Space Agency believe they may have measured the gravitational equivalent of a magnetic field for the first time in a laboratory. Under

> *certain special conditions, the effect is much larger than expected from general relativity and could help physicists to make a significant step toward the long-sought-after quantum theory of gravity..."This experiment is the gravitational analogue of Faraday's electromagnetic induction experiment in 1831. It demonstrates that a superconductive gyroscope is capable of generating a powerful gravitomagnetic field, and is therefore the gravitational counterpart of the magnetic coil. Depending on further confirmation, this effect could form the basis for a new technological domain, which would have numerous applications in space and other high-tech sectors," said ESA study manager Clovis de Matos.*
>
> "Experimental Detection of the Gravitomagnetic London Moment," European Space Agency, March 23, 2006

Fortunately for the rest of the world, ESA's team did not stop with one successful experiment early in the century. By the midtwenties, a European syndicate began marketing an artificial gravity system that could be sized down to the old International Space Station or up to a small asteroid. The system relied on contemporary superconductors and could provide virtually any desired field strength. It completely changed the way designers and planners thought about space stations and colonies, since it obviated the need for spin to create the illusion of gravity.

~

Carolyn's thoughts were interrupted by a Ship's announcement: "Ladies and gentlemen, the landing sequence will commence in eighteen minutes. Please take your seats." As others in the lounge began to settle, she elected to return to her tiny cabin for the maneuver. Despite her continuing avoidance of most higher technology, the years had treated her kindly; she was fit and appeared many years younger than her chronological age. Looking forward to her new life, she was also quite alone.

Five minutes later a faint vibration was evident as braking and docking jets fired. On impulse, she addressed the shipboard Artificial Intelligence:

"Ship, may I ask you a question?"

"Of course, Ms. West," came the reply. The Ship had spoken only briefly when they had departed GEO station, and she had kept to herself most of the intervening four months.

"How long have you been making this trip back and forth to Eros?"

After a brief pause, which she assumed was for her benefit, the disembodied but warm voice spoke: "I have been involved in the solar transit program since its inception in 2029, and I have been a class-III ferry since 2045." Carolyn was stunned. That could only mean...

Ship continued, "I was originally a biological human, one of the engineers who worked on the first ferry designs and construction. In 2045, I had the opportunity to upload. I've never been sorry, although I do miss a good steak now and then."

Carolyn was dimly aware of additional vibration and noises through the hull, but her consciousness had sharpened to a razor-thin focus on the Ship. She knew of uploads, of course. They had been common in society for decades. But she had never met or conversed with one before, had in fact avoided them at all costs once she began losing friends and family to the process.

Ship spoke again: "Ms. West, your aversion to my form of life is well known among us. We all regret it, but none of us has a solution. I hope you're prepared for what awaits you on Eros, because there it will be much more difficult for you to avoid nonbiological life." Ship's voice changed subtly, and Carolyn dimly realized it was now making an announcement."

Ladies and gentlemen, we are now ready for you to disembark. Please proceed to the departure lounge."

Standing, she headed out the door and down the corridor. Behind her, Ship said, "Good luck, Ms. West."

3

Deep space, the far side of Jupiter and ten degrees above the ecliptic. Except for an occasional particle, virtually nothing disturbs the vacuum. The Sun is a bright but distant speck. The nearest matter of any consequence is many millions of miles away.

A pinpoint of light grows, indicating movement toward the inner solar system. The image resolves into a spherical construct, outwardly metallic, covered by a variety of small forms whose functions can only be guessed. Propulsion, of course, and perhaps communications, but mysteries enshroud the rest. Its size becomes apparent, and it measures nearly ten kilometers in diameter—which means that something is occupying over five hundred cubic kilometers within.

On close examination, the outer shell appears to continually shift and re-form in subtle ways. There is no obvious mechanism by which this occurs. Projections variously appear, morph, and disappear while color and texture undergo ceaseless permutation.

Whatever its origin, whatever its purpose, one thing is clear: the construct and whatever it holds are in a *hurry*. It has already achieved speed far greater than is ever seen in the inner solar system, and it is still accelerating. One wonders how, if it has an inner-system destination in mind, it will manage to shed enough delta-v to achieve orbit, but its guiding intelligence is apparently unconcerned.

As it passes, the construct's general features settle into a new pattern. It bears a disturbing resemblance to a being out of human religious folklore, a creature neither seen nor heard from in centuries.

4

Captain Jack was quite pleased with himself. Over the years that he'd been taking fishing charters out on Lake Ontario, he had seen firsthand the inexorable shift of game species farther and farther offshore, many of them ultimately disappearing. He and his fellow guides had found it increasingly difficult to provide their clients with a satisfactory fishing experience. The lake itself had changed, shrinking as the world warmed. Dredging now went on practically nonstop in the Genesee River and nearby bays.

Today, however, the rangy, weather-beaten guide was back in business and quite pleased with himself. The first run of the day had been uneventful. Starting fifteen miles directly off Irondequoit Bay, he had trolled east into the rising sun at two knots, lines out, sensors on. His four customers variously sat or stood on the rear deck nursing morning-after coffees while Ed, his deckhand, attended to the rigging. Two miles into the run, Jack pressed an inconspicuous button set under the Larson's control panel. Portside, just above the waterline, several gallons of gray fluid drained through an outlet in the hull into the lake. The fluid contained billions of molecular sensors designed to find and attach themselves to salmon and lake trout. They were not legal. But Captain Jack no longer cared—he knew he needed an edge or he would soon be out of business, and the Asian firm that had sold him the nanosystem was unconcerned with its application.

~

In the early days of white settlement around Lake Ontario, the native Atlantic salmon was an irresistible source of food and recreation. Speared and netted nearly to extinction, the once-abundant fish all but disappeared by 1900. Dams, pollution, and runoff made natural recovery impossible. Aggressive restocking during the twentieth and twenty-first centuries finally reestablished the species, though little natural propagation had taken hold.

Silvery, metallic, and streamlined, the salmon moved slowly through the dark waters over one hundred feet below the surface. For some days its primitive brain had been registering hunger. It had just fed, savaging a young alewife with its powerful jaws, but that tasty morsel had merely taken the edge off. It would need much, much more. Soon.

Dimly aware of throaty engine noise passing overhead, it flicked its tail in annoyance and began a leisurely swim away. The noise eventually faded as the fish drifted through the blue-green gloom in search of prey.

It was still searching an hour later when the aggravating noise returned. About to head into deeper waters, it glimpsed a slowly moving creature passing nearby. Unsure but interested, the salmon circled to come up behind in stalking position before spotting the cable. Something was wrong.

Before it could drop back and head the other way, the fish was nearly convulsed with intense hunger. Cable be damned!

~

Things began to happen fast on the return leg. By the time the thirty-two-foot Larson had made its turn and returned to the release area, the microscopic sensors had been working for over an hour. A receiving module picked up their signals, processed them for the most likely targets, and directed the autopilot to guide the boat on the most auspicious vector. As the Larson moved into position, the module directly geared the lines up or down to the appropriate depths, ensuring that the nearly irresistible lures passed within inches of the targets. As a further hedge, Jack had purchased a blend; the sensor nanobots were accompanied by Cravers. These microscopic injectors triggered the hunter-hunger reflex in any fish that happened to be near a passing lure. The fish, of course, never had a chance.

~

One hundred twenty feet below the surface, the now-ravenous salmon accelerated swiftly as it opened massive jaws in anticipation of the meal to come. A day earlier, Ed the deckhand had spent the afternoon sharpening single-, double-, and treble-hooked lures with a stone made for just that purpose. When its mouth snapped shut, the salmon was pierced so cleanly that at first it felt nothing but the metal in its mouth. Then came the pain, and the anger.

Hangovers forgotten, the four customers whooped and cheered as the enormous Atlantic salmon leapt right out of the water in a futile attempt to shake loose of the lure. First one, then another reeled in trout and salmon worthy of any display wall. Ed worked nonstop to get the fish in the boat and reset the lines. Resettling his hat, Captain Jack lit up a Cuban and leaned back in his chair. He smiled at the mayhem, quite pleased with himself and wondering what had taken him so long to figure out what to do. He had watched as one after another of his friends had sold their rigs and left the lake for other pursuits, and he had known for a long time that his turn was coming without drastic action.

Better later than never, he thought with satisfaction. Now it was midafternoon and the Larson was just re-entering the mouth of the Genesee River. His rather comatose charges had all limited (of course) and then proceeded to drink all the beer on board. No matter. The tips would be good, and word of mouth would ensure additional business. As they passed the newly refurbished ferry terminal, Jack noticed the potted palm trees lining the waterfront. People were boarding the ferry for the one-hour ride to Toronto, which had become quite the tourist destination with the arrival of the tropics in the Great Lakes.

"Captain, we may have a problem." The normally taciturn Ed had come up to the bridge with a troubled look on his face.

"Talk to me, Eddie." Jack had taken Ed into his confidence when planning the nanosystem, since there would have been no fooling the man once fish started to appear. Ed had appeared unconcerned at the time, merely nodding in acquiescence.

"I overheard two of the customers talking, and one guy was, ah, suspicious about their good luck."

"Don't let it worry you. What's he going to do, tell the Coast Guard he caught too many fish?"

"Maybe he already has," Ed replied as he got up to help with the docking. As Jack maneuvered the boat into Slip 157, he was aware of two uniformed men watching them approach. One wore Coast Guard blue, and the other appeared to be a state conservation officer. The men caught the lines Ed tossed from bow and stern, and then expertly secured the boat to cleats on the dock.

"Captain Anders?" asked one of the men. Jack nodded his head. "Captain, I'm going to have to ask you to come with us. I will not arrest you at this time if you come along voluntarily."

"May I ask why?"

The officer replied, "We have received a report of illegal technology use and need to ask you and your associate some questions. We will also be impounding your boat." At which point Jack noticed a white van bearing law enforcement insignia driving up to the slip. It disgorged three white-suited technicians carrying cases.

With a sick feeling in the pit of his stomach, Jack turned to Ed and shrugged apologetically before following the officer to the waiting transport.

~

Three days later, Jack Anders used the last of his meager savings to board a flight for Quito. The hearing officer had been quite specific; he faced extensive jail time, or he could accept emigration to an asteroid. No choice at all, really, and Jack was unsurprised when Kathy informed him he was on his own. She had grown quite distant as his business had worsened, though he had to admit it was at least as much his fault as hers. Hard times had revealed his brooding, morose side. At least the kids were grown and gone, and he knew Kathy would have no trouble establishing herself in a new life that excluded Jack Anders.

Once in Quito, he reported to the sprawling Resettlement Authority complex for assignment. He found he didn't care much about the details; his life as he had experienced it was over, and whatever the future held, it was unknowable. The Resettlement AI informed him that he would be leaving on the very next elevator for GEO station and gave him both his electronic ticket and destination packet. Carrying his duffel, Jack headed for the departure lounge.

5

Much had changed in the century since the original International Space Station had been assembled in orbit. For one thing, the GEO stations were 23,000 miles up, not the 220 or so miles of the early station. For another, the GEOs, particularly those that handled most of the passenger traffic (Quito, Kisumu, and Pekanbaru), were enormous by comparison. Their primary function was to serve as intermodal transit nodes. This required a combination of services that had been present at such points throughout history—traffic control, lodging, dining, shopping, health care, and so on. And the less savory as well, although the authorities attempted to keep a tight rein on vice. On any given day, hundreds of people were likely to be present both in GEO's giant cylinder and in the nearby Marriott and Hilton hotels.

The papal "elevator" arrived at midday station's time, and virtually the entire crew and transient population were present to welcome the pontiff and his entourage. The arrival lounge itself was not especially large, but the connecting hallway was wide and enabled bystanders to line up on either side. Gravity in this area was maintained near Earth-normal to make it easier for new arrivals to acclimate. As the pope stepped into the lounge, he was greeted by the stationmaster, Colonel

Jorge Herrera. Everyone took note of the pope's failure to kiss the "ground" as he often did when arriving at terrestrial destinations; after all, how could the station floor be said to constitute sacred soil? Yet, some in the crowd were disappointed.

Led by station security and his Swiss guard, John XXIV proceeded through the enthusiastic crowd to the maze of corridors and apartments that constituted the station's residential district. After taking his leave, Colonel Herrera returned to his post, shaking his head at the fickleness of human nature. He well knew that most in the crowd were reacting to the pope's celebrity and had absolutely no interest in the teachings or beliefs he espoused. *Not my problem,* he thought as he re-entered the command center.

Arriving at the residential area, the pope and his associates were shown to a suite occupying nearly half of an entire level of the cylindrical module. While the quarters were somewhat cramped, they were quite secure and isolated from the noise generated by the business of the station's daily routine. More luxurious accommodations were available in the nearby commercial hotels but had been deemed more vulnerable. For once, John XXIV had agreed with his staff. He had no wish to call more attention to himself than was necessary until he was ready to do so.

"Alberto," he addressed Father Bertani, "please check with whomever is necessary and find out when our ferry and its pilot will be available. I would like to talk with the pilot *in person* as soon as possible."

"Si, Holiness," Bertani replied as he finished unpacking and stowing the pope's luggage.

As the young priest turned to leave, John XXIV said, "And Alberto? Give me two hours, please. Let the good eminences know that I wish to meditate and pray and would prefer not to be disturbed."

"Of course, Holy Father." With that, Father Bertani left, and the pope was alone for the first time in nearly eight days.

He kneeled at the prie-dieu that always traveled with him—a gift from his parents upon his ordination. Quite unremarkable, quite worn, and perhaps the only material possession he felt any attachment to, the antique rosewood and velour comforted him. He cleared his mind and prayed for guidance. Sound and sight faded from his consciousness as he allowed his passion to suffuse his awareness.

Dimly, he was aware of the passage of time. For perhaps the thousandth time, he acknowledged his weaknesses, especially the self-doubt that sometimes left him nearly paralyzed. He knew he needed help to accomplish his goals, help that he'd been able to find nowhere in the Church. He prayed further that what he was about to do would not damn his immortal soul. He took hold of the simple wooden cross that always hung about his neck, turned it over, and used a fingernail to slide a panel on the rear open. It was a moment's work to press the button concealed within, observe the glow of a tiny LED, and slide the cover back into place. He resumed his meditations.

Billions of nanites nestled deep within the pope's central nervous system woke up when he triggered the electronic signal. They had been "installed" at the time of his treatment years earlier for bone cancer, first entering his bloodstream and then migrating to their destinations. At something like twenty-six hundred to the inch, they were undetectable except with advanced instrumentation; however, each had the ability to supercharge its host neuron by vastly speeding up the electrochemical transactions that constituted physical and mental processing. Quiescent until activated, their energy source was the adenosine triphosphate that already fueled many of the body's cellular mechanics.

John XXIV was unaware of all of this. His thoughts were focused and clear, and they were thoughts of how he had come to this place. He had decided, finally, that the direction of the Church and of civilization was unmistakable. The twenty-first-century Church had become so marginalized by the close of the century that its prelate no longer figured in daily public discourse. John had concluded that he had no choice but to join with the revolution sweeping humanity into the uncertain future. The only way he could guide it would be from within.

The tinnitus that engendered the background noise he had lived with for years seemed suddenly to intensify. Shaking his head, he thought briefly of earplugs before realizing the noise was actually dissipating. He found he could discern sounds that evidently had been with him all along. Sounds like the beating of his heart.

Opening his eyes, he saw everything he looked at with clarity. His refraction had been compromised by middle age, resulting in nearsightedness that he corrected with old-fashioned glasses that were currently in his pocket. He blinked. He shook his head again, rubbed his eyes. He realized he could see minute dimples on the walls and ceilings, fine lines in the door's wood laminate. Tiny words printed on a label affixed to the closet door were legible, seemingly magnified as he glanced at them.

The ambivalent feelings of hesitation and reluctance John had been living with were gone, banished by a newfound contextual awareness. He remembered everything in a multitiered hyperknowledge that allowed both analog association and digital reduction. He found he could control his scattered thoughts by willing them to sharpen their focus on people, places, events. He began to feel astonishment, and hope.

Eventually, his gaze settled on the wall-hung ship's clock, a relic from simpler times, and he realized the second hand had slowed perceptibly. In fact, it barely moved.

He understood immediately that his temporal sense had shifted as his mental processes had accelerated. John felt a slight stirring of doubt as his thoughts raced ahead; given such a basic discontinuity, how could anyone live in the real world with ordinary people? He trembled at the thought that in his hubris he might have erred after all. Sweat beaded on his forehead. He closed his eyes, only to snap them open when a knock sounded at the door.

By the clock, Bertani had departed less than an hour earlier, so it could not be his assistant. Who would dare disturb the pope? Barely able to speak, John said, "Enter, if you must."

The door swung open, and Cardinal Rauschman strode into the room.

6

Palermo, Italy, 1801—As he made his way through the royal palace on New Year's Day, the middle-aged priest reflected on the excesses of the previous evening. *Something about the turning of the year at the beginning of a century,* he mused. It had turned otherwise sensible people into lunatics who imbibed, reveled, and debauched themselves into exhaustion. Very few were about even now at the dinner hour. Father Giuseppe Piazzi knew he would need to put in extra cathedral time hearing confessions for the next few days, but right now he was driven by the brilliant winter skies to the observatory. Perched atop the tower of Santa Ninfa, the Palermo Circle was a modified theodolite whose brass structure supported a five-foot vertical circle. It was widely held to be the most accurate star-gazing instrument of the day. Piazzi had worked hard to bring the observatory into being, and he worked just as hard to maintain it in the face of academic jealousy and an indifferent king.

As he and his assistant worked on his star catalog, he made an entry noting the presence of a tiny star in the shoulder of the constellation Taurus. When he returned to it the following night to verify its position, he found to his surprise that it had moved. Muttering about "mistakes," he noted the corrected position. Two nights later, however, there was no longer any doubt that the object was moving, which indicated that a new comet must be at hand even though no halo was visible. Father Piazzi notified the press. As he and the rest of the world soon learned, his discovery of Ceres revealed a whole new class of celestial bodies.

Two hundred and five years later, the International Astronomical Union reclassified Ceres as a "dwarf planet," bringing it to the public's attention for the first time in many years and giving new impetus to an exploratory mission on the drawing boards at NASA.

Nine years later, Ceres had a visitor. After an extended journey that included a flyby of Mars and a seven-month stop at Vesta, a robotic spacecraft arrived to get acquainted.

> *PASADENA, Calif. – Scientists at the Jet Propulsion Laboratory and UCLA released the first close-up photographs of Ceres, once the largest asteroid and now perhaps the smallest planet. Taken by the Dawn spacecraft, the photos show a rocky, primitive surface pockmarked by impact craters. They also show what appear to be small polar ice caps.*

> *Mission Scientist Dr. Chris Russell cautioned against any early conclusions, saying only, "We are excited by the quality of the data we are receiving. We should be able to fully characterize Ceres as long as Dawn keeps transmitting."*
> *New York Times,* February 16, 2015

For five months Dawn's cameras, lasers, spectrometers, and more esoteric instrumentation probed the asteroid, ultimately from low orbit. They confirmed some details and added many more. With a diameter of roughly six hundred miles, the asteroid's surface area to be mapped was over 40 percent the size of the continental United States. Its stony soils include minerals, hydrates, and ice. It rotates in just over nine hours, and its gravity is 3 percent of Earth-normal.

~

Thirty-six years after Dawn departed for an extended tour of the asteroid belt, the first humans reached Ceres on September 1, 2051. Taking months instead of years, their craft and two accompanying tugs delivered them with a combination of technology and supplies designed to make feasible construction of a permanent habitat. There was no going back. This first group of volunteers knew they were making a one-way trip, at least until a future Ceres-based enterprise could launch its own ferries. Or until more visitors arrived.

Within three months they had completed a space elevator, a relatively simple task in Ceres' low-gravity environment. Their passenger craft became their GEO station, and traffic began flowing back and forth to the surface only 486 miles below, where they named the ground station Piazzi. In three more months they had extended the settlement both on the surface and below ground, where their task was to determine whether tunneling with modified nanobots could be accomplished with reasonable effort. It could. Miles of tunnels, chambers, and vaults began to take shape; the news reported back to Earth, Mars, and the Moon gave a renewed focus to the frenzy of planning and shipbuilding that had been going nonstop for almost twenty years. The largest emigration in history had commenced with the first passenger space elevator operations, and Ceres would become the next destination of choice.

One year after the first volunteer crew arrived, ferries began to arrive at GEO Station Piazzi on a regular basis. Most of the new arrivals were boomers looking to escape the deteriorating circumstances on Earth, though occasionally there were younger people. Once in a while, a pre-boomer who managed to survive into the era of advanced medicine would also show up, though these individuals were rare. At peak, as many as 40,000 relocated to Ceres each year. By the time of John XXIV's arrival at GEO Station Kisumu, 3.4 million people called Ceres home.

These mostly boomer Ceresians were attracted by the asteroid's size, which made possible the dwelling of one's choice, and by its location in the belt. Water, carbon, and metals were abundant. Ceres was the ideal staging area for explorers, miners, and the attendant service industries, since something like 15 percent of all asteroids were within sixty degrees including some of the larger, more interesting specimens such as Thisbe and Laetitia. Commerce blossomed.

Ceres was attractive for another reason as well; from day one, human and machine civilizations were fully integrated. The pioneer crew had been accompanied by two advanced IBM Crays whose AI potential far outstripped anything else currently deployed off-Earth. One had been installed on the new GEO station, and the other took up residence several months later in the subterranean recesses of Piazzi. They became the principal nodes of the Ceresweb, which ultimately encompassed the entire planetoid and nearby space. All arriving settlers were linked through nanotechnology or older-style macroenhancements. Security, life support, business, communications—all became superefficient and ubiquitous as a result.

The choices available to Ceresians in their daily and long-term pursuits were practically unlimited. Virtual reality complemented "real" reality. The line between artificial intelligence and human intelligence, already indistinct, disappeared as knowledge multiplied and innovation became routine. Many Ceresians adapted the human physique to their new world's conditions, and the results were sometimes surprising.

And one more thing: on Ceres, no one ever died.

7

Perhaps more interesting than this scanning-the-brain-to-understand-it approach would be scanning the brain for the purpose of downloading it. We would map the locations, interconnections, and contents of all the neurons, synapses, and neurotransmitter concentrations. The entire organization, including the brain's memory, would then be recreated on a digital-analog computer.

Ray Kurzweil, "The Coming Merging of Mind and Machine," *Scientific American*, September 1, 1999.

HARTFORD, Conn. – Insurance giant Aetna Life & Casualty unveiled a new product it called "Enduring Life" today. Senior Vice President Rachel Curtis described it this way: "Enduring Life enables our customers for the first time to protect themselves against accidental death for one affordable prepaid premium."

> *The new product assists those who have undergone nanoenhancement of the central nervous system. It provides contingentprogrammingandasubdermal "escape module" in which neurobots collect in the event of systemic biologic failure. The module is then removed for uploading or transfer to another host.*
>
> *Consumer advocates were quick to point outthatAetna'sviewof"affordable"wasat considerable variance with conventional wisdom.*
>
> *Wall Street Journal, April 27, 2060*

Practically no one came to Ceres (or any other off-planet) destination unenhanced. Aging boomers, in particular, were both able to afford the technology and in dire need of its rejuvenating consequences, if not its expansion of mental power. The same people were quick to ensure that the insurance industry's modified life-extension product became a success. Ceres provided the ideal environment to perfect the system.

Because humans and machines were integrated, the location and condition of each individual was always known. When the infrequent catastrophic accidents occurred, the victims were recovered immediately and uploaded into the planet's now-massive data storage and processing media. In effect, Ceres itself became a giant computer with multiple intelligences who sometimes merged and sometimes went their own ways.

Despite the electronic backup, most Ceresians were quite individual in their varied approaches to life. The settlers had come a long way to have things their way. The asteroid's size gave them the ability to do just that, and it was not unusual to see the children of the sixties living alone, or in small communes, or in other unconventional arrangements not common on Earth.

8

It was just a different sort of place. Carolyn found upon entry that she had no choice about one very basic quality-of-life decision: all settlers on and in Eros acquired a full complement of nanites, neurobots, respirocytes, and other advanced maintenance and medical nanorobots within minutes. They permeated the rocky environment. She had managed to overlook this aspect of Erosan life during her researches, and her new passengers went to work as she cleared customs and went looking for the resettlement office. Thus ended the decades she had spent avoiding the technology.

Carolyn left the Resettlement AI and headed for her temporary quarters accompanied by a human guide, an apparently older man whose name tag read "Arthur." Their small electric vehicle followed a broad, winding corridor that appeared to be paved with brick, occasionally traversing the network of cavernous enclaves that honeycombed this part of Eros. Arthur pointed out landmarks and described the activities within. One of the first settled asteroids, Eros was known for its dedication to learning and research. Many of Earth's great institutions had extensions on Eros, and Carolyn was bemused by their retro appearance that utilized columns, porticos, windows, and even something looking like ivy that graced the local establishments.

The people she saw looked purposeful. Some had the obvious, older-style macroenhancements. Many smiled and gave small waves as they passed, and Carolyn began to feel unexpectedly buoyant and carefree. She found herself quite taken by the unforced enthusiasm in Arthur's voice; so much so, in fact, that her awareness of the passing landscape dimmed as she studied his face while he spoke. The few lines seemed to give him character. The texture of his skin seemed important for some reason. She began to *see*.

Attentive, Arthur became aware of the change in his charge. As they entered her quarters in the residential district he said, "Miss West, may I ask how you are feeling right now?"

Carolyn heard his words clearly and opened her mouth to answer, then stopped; her mind was a beehive. Thousands of thoughts and memories fought for attention. She looked at Arthur, unable to speak.

He recognized what was happening to her, having witnessed it before and been trained in how to respond. "Miss West, I see that you are new to nanoenhancement. Please close your eyes and listen carefully to my voice." Trembling, she complied.

"Rarely, someone comes to Eros who has no experience with advanced molecular nanotechnology. Not often, but it does happen, as you are experiencing now. As you are no doubt aware, this technology confers many benefits but also comes with a challenge: you must learn to direct it. Uncontrolled, it will extend your life and keep your body healthy, but your mind will retreat into a randomized catatonia from which you may never recover."

Now Arthur took Carolyn's hands in his own. "Carolyn, I must ask you to trust me a bit, though you and I have just met. There is not enough time for proper medical intervention. If you permit, I will transfer a sufficient number of my own neurobots to you to provide the requisite control instruction-sets to your own. I would not otherwise invade your privacy this way, but there is no alternative if we are to preserve your sanity."

Carolyn nodded her head. She could almost feel her mind struggling to skitter away, and the thought that it might succeed terrified her far more than any alternative she could imagine.

Leading her by the hand, Arthur drew her into the sleeping quarters and down onto the bed. She tried to help, but the terror consuming her mind made her efforts feeble at best. He was as gentle as she knew he would be, and she found her body responding in spite of the fear. When it was over she lay in his arms, her thoughts finally sorting and crystallizing into a new hyperawareness.

"Is this the way you welcome all your new ladies?"

"Only those who come unprepared for what we have to offer and need immediate attention," he replied. "They really are few and far between."

Head on hand, she looked at him in some wonder. "Why does it ever happen though? I mean, I should talk, but in this age it seems absurd that anyone ever gets that far. This is the only way to deal with it?"

Looking at her steadily, he was unapologetic. "I can't answer your first question. As to the second, well, this *is* Eros."

9

No-longer-captain Jack had always known in the back of his mind somewhere that inner-system ferry rides meant either interminable boredom or suspended animation for the passengers. He found he was unprepared for the reality, however. Once his elevator arrived at GEO Station Quito, he made his way through the hectic bustle of the transient sector following directions to the departure area, which he found readily enough. Boarding his ship, he was asked to choose an option by the uniformed steward. He had no real choice, since the cost to remain awake, fed, and entertained was beyond his limited means, but his apprehension grew as the preparations for "downtime" proceeded. Struggling for composure, he made conversation with the steward.

"Say, can you tell me how long we'll be in transit? And for that matter, where we're going? I haven't even looked at my resettlement warrant."

The steward replied, "On this run we'll make seven stops over the next eight months. Look at the inside cover of your warrant—what's listed?"

Jack opened the document and read, "TPUD-001. Isn't that an odd name for an asteroid?"

Facing away as he engaged the initiating controls on Jack's cocoon-like downtime bed, the steward hesitated briefly before saying, "The designators changed about twenty years ago when the Inner System Protocols were adopted. Your new home was named under the new system, which gives naming rights to owners and settlers."

As Jack hesitantly folded his long frame into the "bed," he realized that the steward was smiling. Before he could ask why, the steward said, "We'll be about three months getting to your new home, so lie back and enjoy the ride. First, though, drink this." He handed Jack a squeeze bottle full of dark fluid, which Jack found not unpleasant to taste.

As he took the bottle away and closed the lid, the steward said, "Those little 'bots will keep your systems shipshape while you dream away. See you in three months." The transparent lid closed with finality, and Jack felt his unease give way to pleasant lassitude, which faded quickly to nothing at all.

The steward moved on to his next charge after scrawling a note on the bed's cover. It read, simply, "Don."

10

First colonized at around the same time as Ceres, tiny Phobos attracted scientific interest both because of its unique composition and its proximity to Mars. Expeditions to the surface of the "red planet" were few and far between in the early colonial days; there was no easy way to carry enough fuel to ensure one's return, and no apparent way to fabricate any on the surface. So, Phobos became a hub of early boomer settlement, though not to the same extent as Ceres.

Phobos became a trendy new home for settlers from the American West Coast, who were used to living with the imminence of earthquake and tsunami disaster. The tiny moon's orbit is so close to the surface of Mars (less than 4,000 miles) that it loses about 1.8 meters per century as it whirls around the planet. Phobos is doomed, and its doom proved irresistible to the children of Southern California. By the time John XXIV began his historic trip, nearly three hundred thousand occupied the irregular, fourteen-mile-wide sphere.

As on Ceres, an integrated civilization evolved based on human adaptability and advanced technology. Phobos was similarly a center of logistic support, though primarily for those traveling to and from Mars.

Near the close of the twenty-first century, some had begun to propose the concept of moving Phobos into geosynchronous orbit. Mars had yet to construct its own space elevator, and what better GEO station anchor could there be than a moon? The engineering details were ambitious but straightforward.

Predictably, many of the early settlers resisted the idea—after all, it was the inevitable destruction that had brought them to Phobos. Wiser heads prevailed, and by 2103 preparations were under way. Phobos would be moved.

All Martian traffic control was handled through Phobos Center, a multilevel warren of surface and subterranean habitats clustered along the rim of a large crater. Named for the wife of the moon's discoverer, Stickney provided both topographic relief and access to the interior, which turned out to contain caverns in great numbers chock-full of life-giving ice.

There was no real "day" or "night" on Phobos, since the moon raced around Mars more than twice each day. The second shift of Friday, July 20, 2103, brought Chief Controller Meredith Sansone on duty in Phobos Center. The raven-haired technocrat was about as enhanced as a biological human could be, having decided for career reasons to embrace all nano and macro upgrades as soon as they became available. She was not yet ready to upload but was thinking about it. She was one of the elite—a walking, talking biological personality who had no difficulty integrating at will with her AI colleagues, qualities that uniquely suited her to the mental gymnastics of four-dimensional traffic control.

Settling into the command chair at Central Hub, Sansone's piercing blue eyes glanced around briefly before engaging the primary AI interface. She sat on a raised dais which overlooked an open area crowded with workstations where subordinates variously spoke in low tones or sat swathed in virtual reality gear. Vertical surfaces were covered with flat-screen displays, and holographs floated nearby. The entire hub seemed to hum with purpose. She allowed herself a small smile. *Not bad for South Carolina trailer trash*, she thought as she slipped on her headset and entered VR.

Her senses immediately expanded "outward" as she became one with the electronic Phobos. Nanosensors fed a constant stream of situational data to her while traffic control tracked all inbound, outbound, and transient activity in Martian space. She was able to "zoom" in to any data stream that triggered warnings. Like all good managers, her chief function was to delegate situations or at least to make sure the AI autoroutines were addressing each such need. After thirty minutes of concentrated effort, she was satisfied that all systems were working properly. She settled into her normal shift routine, allowing the AI to carry on while she focused more or less randomly on various system elements: the position of Deimos, a departing ferry, a nearby asteroid, a freighter inbound from the belt. Time passed.

Three hours into the shift she became aware of an anomaly. An intermittent return signal had appeared at the extreme edge of her sensor range, well above the ecliptic. This was not unusual; the inner solar system was full of signal and noise generators of all types. Its apparent position was a bit odd, but she dismissed it from her mind as the AI routed it to one of her deputies for monitoring.

An hour later, the same deputy took the extraordinary step of asking for a real-world conversation. Most controllers spent their entire shifts in virtual reality except for meal breaks. She was so surprised she forgot to be annoyed with the interruption and agreed. The young deputy mounted the dais holding hard copy—also extraordinary—and Sansone began to feel worry.

She snapped, "Talk to me, Robert. We both know this better be good."

"Chief, we've been tracking an intermittent for the past hour, and it's showing characteristics we're unable to classify. It appears to be moving faster than anything this far in should be moving. It may be big. And it seems to be coming this way." He handed her the copy, which showed only a rather indistinct disc.

"This is the best we can do," he continued, "since the returns continue to vary all over the place. We should have something clearer in twenty minutes." The disc appeared to have texture, but no details were evident.

The fact that it was heading toward Martian space was troubling, but Meredith was more troubled by its vector; it seemed to be coming from a nowhere location in deep space. And there was no doubt about it; it had to be artificial.

She said, "Come see me again when you have more, and make sure our friends down below are aware of it." Robert hurried off to contact the main observatory on Mars.

Thirty minutes later he was back, ashen-faced as he handed her another image. She took a long, hard look at it, then him, and then said, "This isn't some kind of practical joke, right?" Having trouble speaking, he swallowed and mopped his forehead.

He finally managed, "Chief, this is what we get combining our feeds with Deimos and the groundside observatory. If it's a joke, someone is manipulating an awful lot of data."

Meredith said, "Put a real-time feed on the main screen."

Robert hustled back to his station and made it happen, whereupon activity in the hub ground to a halt as all eyes turned to the image. The previously hazy disc had resolved into what almost appeared to be a face.

Robert said, "Whatever it is, it will be here in forty-five minutes, Chief."

ARLINGTON, Va. – The Defense Advanced Research Projects Agency (DARPA) today announced the third round of its competition to develop the technology behind the Pulsed Harmonic Assembler Strategic Energy Ray. Agency Director Dr. Michael Exton said, "We learned a great deal from PHASER's first two rounds. I'm optimistic that recent developments in superconductor technology will now be applied to PHASER. We expect to have a workable prototype within five years."

DARPA will award prizes for the top three designs, as evidenced by working prototypes. The winner will receive $3 million, second prize is $1.5 million, and third prize is $500,000.

New York Times, March 14, 2039

Not quite forty-five minutes later, Meredith, Robert, and every other pair of human and electronic eyes watched as the sphere whipped around Mars to pass close by Phobos. They had determined size, mass, density, and other measurable characteristics. No hailing on any frequency evoked a response. *NOW what?* wondered Meredith.

That question was soon answered. As the sphere made its closest approach, sensors observed its release of a ball of light in the direction of Phobos. Traveling swiftly, the ball expanded upon impact and engulfed the tiny moon.

> *WASHINGTON, D.C. – Frankenstein's man-made monster of Mary Shelley's classic horror tale seems to be lumbering after proponents of nanotechnology.*
>
> *The creature has been evoked by people fearful that the hot technology of the twenty-first century will run amok. This time, the torch-bearing villagers are gathering around the "gray goo" menace, fearful that self-replicating, biological nanomachines ceaselessly will reproduce and take over the world.*
>
> *Nanotechnology pioneer K. Eric Drexler first warned of gray goo in his 1986 book Engines of Creation. Nanomachines "could spread like blowing pollen, replicate swiftly and reduce the biosphere to dust in a matter of days," he wrote.*
>
> *USA Today, September 27, 2004*

Back in AI harness, Meredith's first impression of the impact was of a faint vibratory buzz. She knew almost immediately what was happening; trillions of trillions of molecular reducers were at work churning through the stuff of Phobos, replicating themselves as they went. The outer crust of the moon, including all surface facilities, was reduced to ash in seconds. Phobos' powerful AI core extrapolated consequences and immediately reprogrammed defensive nanobots to counter the assault. As Meredith "watched" in virtual reality, the defenders were gobbled up by the leading edge of the ravening attackers as if they had never existed.

On a molecular level, each attacker was equipped with a claw designed to disassemble whatever confronted it. Remarkably efficient, the microscopic berserkers also tore through defenders without pause, even when the AI sent successive waves, reprogrammed to meet the specific threat. The invaders had anticipated all reprogramming.

A scream tore through the hub. Meredith ripped her headset off in time to see the forward wall dissolve, flat panels and all. Pandemonium broke out as her staff began racing for the exits, only to find those walls collapsing as well. And then it began; first one, then another of her people howled in agony as their bodies seemed to disintegrate from their feet up. Frozen to the command chair, she watched Robert slump into a shapeless mound. Moments later she observed her own demise with some detachment. Her last thought as consciousness faded was that her Enduring Life policy was unlikely to be of any help.

11

Many competing undercurrents ran through society in the 2020s and 2030s as advanced medicine and life extension became widespread. Boomers used their rather astonishing wealth to indulge themselves and pursue whatever caught their fancy. Often, their first priority was escape from the social and environmental upheaval endemic to Earth. Others spent fortunes re-engineering their bodies and minds. For millions, though, such ideas conflicted with deeply held beliefs, or at least with psychological constraints disguised as beliefs. For them, relocation to other worlds was unthinkable and life without death was inconceivable. They lived their sometimes very long lives and passed on.

Then there was the communal movement, to which uploading gave a whole new dimension. How better to live in collective harmony than to inhabit cyberspace with your fellows, leading electronic lives in shared virtual worlds? All the New Age drama of the 1960s was reprised as millions elected to leave their older or inconvenient bodies for the pure world of electrons. By 2055, most of the repository data storage was housed in massive Sanctuaries orbiting Earth and Moon. Constructed by the same consortium that had built the space elevators and ferries, they were fully automated and required only occasional service calls by biological humans. By 2058, these collectives had begun to assemble together on the far side of the Moon. Their inhabitants were *bored*, and millions of conversations later they evolved a common goal: galactic exploration. The challenge of the unknown was cause for endless excitement, planning, and speculation as they used robotic technology and materials mined from lunar soil to transform the Sanctuaries into a self-propelled starship. What emerged was a cluster of interconnected modules driven by fusion and solar sails. In 2063 they set out amid much fanfare throughout the Inner System, though in truth no one seemed unhappy about their departure. To those still walking, talking, and breathing, Sanctuary was an uncomfortable presence, the minds within unknowable.

12

Father Bertani's low center of gravity reminded others of a football running back as he hustled down the ferry's main corridor. Having just been instructed by the pontiff to arrange use of the main salon for Mass, he thought again of the strange events surrounding their departure from GEO Station Kisumu and shook his head. When he had returned from his errands, he'd found the pope behind closed doors with Cardinal Rauschman. Unusual, but not unheard of. Then he'd been ordered by Rauschman to run to the medical center and return with a syringe, of all things. When he'd hesitated, Pope John had seconded the order. As he'd made his way back through the station, he picked up the ferry captain, who happily had appeared ahead of schedule. Bertani knew how anxious the Holy Father was to talk with the man, a garrulous, bearded old-timer. But when he returned with a syringe kit borrowed from medical stores, Rauschman sent the captain away as he took the syringe from the priest. Bertani and the captain eyed each other as the door slammed shut.

Finally the captain shrugged and said, "Look me up on the bridge when you need me." Bertani nodded and returned to his quarters, confusion giving way to resignation.

Answering a papal summons the next morning, the priest found the pope in a quiet, almost morose mood as they prepared to embark. On their way to the departure lounge, John XXIV stopped at a conference room that served multiple purposes, including those of the media, and conducted a twenty-minute press conference. The half-dozen reporters asked for trip details and threw in one or two softball questions about Church policy. The ferry would make six stops at major settlements over the next five months before returning to Earth.

When asked again about the underlying purpose of the voyage, John said simply, "We're here because God's love follows his children wherever they go, wherever they live. We have left the homeworld, but we take His teachings with us and must never forget that His values make us greater than we could otherwise be."

On that high-minded note, the press conference ended and the group departed, led by the three burly Swiss guards who had drawn the trip assignment. Once again, Bertani noted the pope's distracted, preoccupied demeanor. One of the Curia members, the rotund Cardinal Thomas Llewellyn of Wales, was attempting without success to draw the pontiff into conversation. The pope waved him off, saying "Later, Eminence."

As the ferry drew away from GEO station, Bertani was struck by how off-center the entire morning, indeed the past twenty-four hours, had been. It culminated with the pope's announcement that there would be no suspended animation, or "downtime," on the trip; he expected that they would all use the transit times to meditate and pray for divine guidance. This drew grumbles, but no one dared defy him openly. Rauschman actually seemed pleased by the prospect.

Now, the trip was three weeks old and they were halfway to their first stop, the odd little world of Eros. After conferring with the captain, Father Bertani began setting up the salon for Mass. The room featured subdued lighting and plain, unadorned walls. Scheduled for an hour later, this had become a daily ritual that attracted most of the ship's passengers and off-duty crew, drawn by the opportunity to hear the pope's homilies on whatever crossed his mind. As he completed the setup, the priest was surprised by an announcement over the ship's system.

"Father Bertani, please report to the bridge."

When he arrived the captain said, "We've just received a distress call," and handed him a transcript. It was a request for aid originating on a small mining asteroid named O'Toole. No details.

The captain continued, "I bring it to your attention only because we're passing within one day's travel, which makes us the only hope these people have. It will cost time, but I can make the stop if you give the order." Bertani didn't have to think about it; he knew what the pope's legendary compassion would dictate in these circumstances.

"Make the stop, Captain. I'll inform His Holiness."

~

They were greeted on arrival by a large, rather unkempt-looking miner who, upon seeing the priest, paid brief respects and immediately turned to escort the captain, medical officer, and Father Bertani down a long, rough-hewn corridor. The miner spoke little, saying only, "It may be too late," and similar dire predictions. Sure enough, when the group reached a more spacious cavern crowded with perhaps three dozen people, they heard quiet sobbing as they passed among the bowed heads toward a rocky nook. A very old man occupied the shelf within, laid out in what appeared to be a real wood casket. The medic bent over the prone figure, using a handheld device to check vital signs. He looked up at Bertani and shook his head.

The captain turned to their escort and asked, "What happened here? Who is this gentleman?"

Before the man could answer, a sorrowful woman of indeterminate age said, "He was Daniel O'Toole, founder of this world and friend to us all. And what happened was that he just got tired of living. And now he's gone."

This latter statement evoked renewed sobbing from a number of women, and Bertani flinched as the speaker broke into a long, keening wail. He found himself shouldered out of the way by several large men who were nevertheless gentle with the women. When he realized the men were carrying drinks, he began to wonder just what they had gotten themselves into.

~

John XXIV was restless. Anxious to be under way, he decided to see the problem for himself. He knew some of his agitation was the "buzz" created by the newly enhanced awareness he was still learning to manage. Accompanied by a Swiss guard, he made his way into the complex along the same entry corridor Bertani had followed earlier. As they proceeded, the sound of mournful but enthusiastic singing grew in his ears:

Oh Danny boy, the pipes, the pipes are calling
From glen to glen, and down the mountain side
The summer's gone, and all the flowers are dying
'Tis you, 'tis you must go and I must bide.

Entering a large space, the pope was astonished to see bedlam everywhere. Men, women, and children sat at long tables laden with platters of food and pitchers of drink. Robotic servants dashed in and out of doorways carrying trays. One entire wall was fronted by a dark wooden bar complete with a brass rail, and against another, a group of men stood arm in arm around a crypt singing at the top of their lungs:

But come ye back when summer's in the meadow
Or when the valley's hushed and white with snow

'Tis I'll be here in sunshine or in shadow
Oh Danny boy, oh Danny boy, I love you so.

The singers were accompanied by a woman playing an antique piano nearby. A bemused ferry captain stood back from the fray while a frazzled-looking Father Bertani seemed to be deep in conversation with several black-garbed women. Children were everywhere, rushing about in an excess of youthful exuberance. The noise was deafening.

It may have been the bartender who first spotted the pontiff standing in the doorway in his gleaming white cassock. Certainly his jaw was one of the first to drop open. One by one the diners, mourners, singers, and drinkers began to fall silent as they became aware of their most unusual visitor. When Bertani spotted him, he crossed the room with one of the women in tow.Speaking urgently in a low voice he said, "Holiness, please forgive the confusion. We came too late to help the man in the casket. His name is Daniel O'Toole, and may I present his wife, Colleen."

The tall, gray-haired woman was nearly overwhelmed as she knelt to kiss the Ring of the Fisherman. Looking into her green eyes, John XXIV felt great empathy as he drew her to her feet.

"You have my sincere condolences, Mrs. O'Toole. Please continue with your activities; perhaps in a little while you'll allow me to say a prayer of remembrance?"

"Of course, Holy Father, we would be most honored," she managed to reply before fleeing back to her ladies-in-waiting.

Bertani and the Swiss guard arranged a seat for the pope near one end of a long table not far from the crypt. During the next hour, most of the room's occupants paid their respects, kneeling to kiss the ring and receive papal blessings. The festivities gradually resumed, and the pope watched as the area around the casket filled with mournful men and women, most of whom held glasses.

He heard one of the men say, "Liam, give me a hand here. It's time Danny joined his own party." The two men reached into the casket, took gentle hold of the corpse, and wedged him up into a sitting position with a pillow to cushion the body. Another man wrapped one of the corpse's hands around a glass full of amber liquid, while a third straightened his tie. Then they all stepped back and raised their glasses in a toast offered by one of the men: "With apologies to His Holiness," he nodded to John XXIV, "Danny Boy, may ye be in heaven half an hour before the devil knows you're dead." To various inarticulate but vaguely Celtic-sounding cries, the rest of the group clinked glasses and drank. Off to the side, one of the men gestured to the bartender, who quickly handed over a bottle for passing around. A fair-featured lad of about fourteen years wandered through the crowd offering a tray of pipes, cigars, and snuff. As he was engulfed by a cloud of fragrant smoke, the pope thought, *My God in heaven. I'm in the middle of an Irish wake.*

~

An hour later, the assemblage had devolved into bawling, laughing, shouting, and singing. Father Bertani managed to make his way to the pontiff's side to urge their departure, but he found the pope strangely reluctant to leave. John was finding that his system's background static was feeling more like a background connection, or link, with these unusual people.

He said, "I'm ready now, Alberto, to pay my respects to the departed. See if you can get me to the prie-dieu, please."

With that he rose and followed the priest, who found that the mourners were more than willing to make way for their esteemed guest. Kneeling before the casket, John offered a silent prayer for the departed soul of Daniel O'Toole. Feeling the connection even more intensely, he rose and turned to the now-hushed assembly, looking into the many faces before him.

He began speaking about his reasons for being there, about his fears, and especially about his hopes for humanity. He talked about God's love, about its place everywhere. He concluded by saying he didn't know Daniel O'Toole but did know, based on the love all around him, that he must have been a good man who would be sorely missed.

Finally he said, "I know the rosary is traditional at this time and would be honored to say it with you." Many in the crowd actually took beads out of their pockets.

John opened his mouth, but before he could speak he felt a hand on his arm, and a gravelly voice said, "Beggin' yer pardon, Holy Father, but I've always hated the rosary; it's so damn long. Couldn't ye make it something a wee bit shorter?"

Turning to the casket, he was just in time to see Daniel O'Toole slug down the glass of whiskey in his other hand and shake his head with a whoop!

13

Jack opened his eyes. Muted ceiling lights glowed, and after a moment's confusion he realized downtime must be over. The transparent lid of his cocoon swung open, and he heard the cheery voice of the steward: "Rise and shine, Captain Jack. We'll be at your destination in ninety minutes, and you'll be wanting to hydrate and clean up before you arrive." Jack swung his feet to the floor and stood slowly, amazed that he felt so good. He grabbed his duffel and headed for the comfort facilities.

An hour later, he watched the ferry's docking maneuvers on the main screen in the passenger lounge, where he found to his surprise that he was apparently the only traveler departing at this stop. TPUD-001 proved to be a small, metallic ellipsoid eleven miles in length on its long axis. Reading a gazetteer he'd found in the lounge, Jack learned that the object was a "Near-Earth Asteroid," or NEA in astronomical terms, due to its eccentric path, which actually crossed Earth's orbit every now and then.

Docking complete, Jack watched as robotic carriers off-loaded several supply pallets. When it was his turn, the steward escorted him to the exit.

He said, "We'll be returning this way on the inbound leg in about eight weeks, which should give you time to settle in or decide you want to try somewhere else. Good luck to you." Jack thanked the man and proceeded into TPUD-001.

He was met at the customs and resettlement station by a young woman whose beauty took his breath away and by a somewhat crusty-appearing older man. Jack could not keep his eyes off the woman, who wore a uniform much better than he could remember seeing anywhere else. Her long, blonde hair framed an oval face whose blue eyes reflected awareness and intelligence. And something else as well—amusement, perhaps? The older man was the first to speak.

"We're the welcoming committee, Captain Anders. Meet our chief of resettlement, Angela Ford, and I'm Don Foster, original owner and settler of this world of ours."

Jack took the man's outstretched hand, and then did the same with the resettlement officer.

"Angie will show you to your quarters. When you get comfortable, look me up, and I'll give you the nickel tour." Jack agreed, and then set off with the resettlement chief.

Angela led him down a long corridor that gradually widened into a concourse. Illuminated signs beckoned above the numerous doors, advertising everything from clothing to groceries to hardware. They passed a few other pedestrians bound on errands of their own, and to Jack they appeared perfectly ordinary. Branching tunnels led off to both right and left, and it was into one of these that they turned after walking for ten minutes.

"We're almost there," she said after another minute or two. They reached a row of doors having the appearance of a hotel or motel block, and Angela handed Jack an electronic key along with orientation materials.

"When you're ready for Uncle Don, just ring him up through the Net. He's always connected and will meet you right away." She bid him good-bye and walked back down the corridor.

Jack tried to think of something to say to make her stay or at least give him hope that he'd see her again, but he felt tongue-tied. He was also mystified by the "Uncle Don" comment. Uncle? He watched, feeling mildly confused as she strode back up the corridor.

14

Quentin Adler was not a boomer, thank you very much. Fifth son of a fifth son, he was the product of a cross-cultural experiment conducted by his parents in the 1970s. He'd led a mostly solitary life and had been knocking around the Inner System for many years by the time he found his niche, which turned out not to be truck driver after all but long-distance freighter pilot. Most ore and supply hauling was automated under the supervision of advanced AIs or uploads, but there were still runs that required human hands on the controls from time to time. This was especially true in the thickest parts of the belt and in certain docking situations.

When he wasn't on active duty (in other words, most of the time), Quentin read. He knew it was somewhat anachronistic; with his enhancements, he could access virtually any literature or technical writing instantly. He got great pleasure from folding his oversize frame into a comfortable seat for hours, reading through boxes of books, occasionally smoking a cigar or having a glass of port. He had no interest in the downtime of suspended animation either. The solitude was what he lived for, solitude that often lasted months at a time. His only companion was the ship's cat, Flick.

This run was half over. He had left Pallas six weeks earlier bound for Deimos, a load of nickel and iron destined for the Martian moon's manufacturing hub. The trip had been as uneventful as they all were, with one exception: Sarah Chase.

Quentin had run into the same limit to his freedom that sailors had been finding for millennia, namely, his need to connect with a person of the female persuasion. He had known Sarah for twenty years, seeing her during his semiannual visits to Pallas where she operated a popular restaurant. They had been lovers just once, both fearing hopeless entanglement. In the years since, they had opted for an easy friendship. Sarah was always glad to see him, always sorry to see him leave, and he always looked forward to seeing her. She treated him well, not as the somewhat oafish bumbler his self-image called to mind.

As she had served him coffee just before his most recent departure, she told him she had decided to enter a marriage contract with a local miner. Quentin tried not to look as crushed as he felt when he wished her the best and took his leave. Now at odd times during the run in to Deimos, Quentin found himself wondering about Sarah's life to come and about how his life would change as a result. And about lost opportunity.

He was seated on the roomy bridge in just such an introspective mood when a soft chime called his attention to the external sensors. He crossed to the command chair and slipped his helmet on, flipping mental and macro switches as he went. The "view" in this part of the belt was quite sparse. Contrary to popular belief even in the twenty-second century, the asteroid belt did not teem with swarms of rocky planetoids, and Quentin had no difficulty picking out the source of the sensors' attention. A high-albedo object at some distance appeared to be heading directly for him. Checking, he found that it neither emitted nor responded to any signals.

Over the next half hour, the whatever-it-was drew closer. Quentin adjusted his course twice to ensure proper separation, but the object made its own adjustments to stay with him. His disquiet turning to unease, he made one more course change before giving up. Whatever it was, it wanted to dance. And according to the sensors, it was *big*.

He could see a visible disk growing rapidly and removed his helmet to view the approach on the main screen. Flick jumped up into his lap, aware that something unusual was happening. They watched the disk enlarge and begin to differentiate, taking on the aspect of a face.

"What in seven hells is *that*?" he said aloud. It was indeed a face, though not one he cared to know any better. With growing unease, Quentin quickly composed a brief message and sent a directed burst back toward Pallas, knowing it would be quite some time before anyone heard, much less acknowledged.

Flick howled, a banshee-cat noise that stood the little hairs straight out on the back of his neck. The prickly sensation spread all over his body as Flick howled again, and Quentin blinked hard before realizing that the cat was fading away like a puff of smoke blown by a breeze. He realized that the tingling he'd started feeling was *his* body disappearing, and he cursed the luck that had led him to such an end with an inexplicable, menacing visage watching from his main screen. Awareness fled.

Unknowing and uncaring, freighter DP-040 continued on its way.

15

Once they were away from O'Toole, the ferry made good time getting to the next stage of the papal sojourn. John XXIV intended to bring his message of values and relevance to Eros, long regarded by the Church as a center of secularism and godlessness. It was a bold move fraught with risk; many in the media expected the Eros stop to be a disaster from which the trip would not recover.

In his cabin, the pope found that the more he forced his attentions forward, the more they took him back to O'Toole and the pandemonium of their departure. Daniel O'Toole's apparent resurrection had been followed by shrieks, shouts, fainting, shoving, and ultimately by more drinking, singing, eating, and dancing, the latter including O'Toole himself dancing a jig in his own coffin. Before his minders could intervene, John found himself hoisted aloft by two massive miners and carried through the crowd to the relative safety of a small stage, where Bertani and the others finally caught up with him.

"Holy Father, I—" Bertani, it seemed was as speechless as the rest of the group.

Waving the medical officer closer, the pontiff leaned forward urgently and said, "Doctor, what just happened here? You examined the man. What might you have missed?"

The distressed physician said, "Holiness, I cannot say without examining Mr. O'Toole more thoroughly. I can only tell you this, now; he was not breathing, his heart did not beat, he registered no neurological activity. He was clinically dead."

"Alberto," the pope said to Bertani, "return to the ship at once and ask Cardinal Rauschman to join us. Inform him of the events here. We do not have a member of the *Congregatio de Causis Sanctorum* with us, but Josef will be a more-than-adequate stand-in." Charged with managing the complex process of sainthood, the *Congregatio* was also the Vatican's chief investigator of miracles. Bertani hurried away, while across the room, the festivities continued unabated. O'Toole himself was now standing on the bar playing a concertina and singing. The crowd swirled as dancers flung themselves into furious jigs, hornpipes, circles, and squares. Food and drink were everywhere. Periodically, one of the revelers would swirl near and break off long enough to touch the pontifical robes or to kiss the Fisherman's Ring.

When Bertani had returned with Rauschman, John found he could virtually read the cardinal's mind as he took in the madness of the room. Then he went to work.

John smiled as he remembered the outraged miners following the cardinal quite meekly once they got a good look at him. In the end, though, it was the beleaguered medical officer who identified O'Toole's fourth-generation neurobots as the revivifying agent. They had become dormant upon cessation of metabolic activity. Their "reactivate and repair" instruction-sets had been triggered by the pope's own field, which had come near enough to have an impact when he stood up to lead the rosary. Despite Father Bertani's explanations, however, John XXIV knew that the O'Tooles would always remember the incident in miraculous terms.

Docking at Eros was accomplished with minimal fuss. The pope led his entourage into the asteroid where, contrary to the media's more dire predictions, they were welcomed quite enthusiastically. Crowds lined the way as small electric carts transported them to their hotel, and John felt a hyperconscious connection to these people in a way he could not yet define. He'd been nurturing cautious hope for weeks. Now he felt the beginnings of optimism, and it lifted his spirit.

A virtual roundtable was the principal scheduled activity on this stop. Oxford University's Extension College had invited the pope to participate in a conversation with senior faculty. John had no wish to engage in intellectual swordplay but did view the event as an opportunity. He would be using his new connectivity to promote his agenda on the grounds of the oldest university in the English-speaking world; by some accounts, Oxford's beginnings dated back to the reign of William the Conqueror. To prepare himself, he had scheduled a virtual session with Rauschman for later that morning.

Rauschman arrived at 11:30 local time, wearing his habitual scowl. Following the cardinal's lead, the pope took a seat and donned a VR headset. His resident neurobots made gloves and other macro input-output devices unnecessary.

"Holiness, the key is clear instruction," Rauschman said. "It is always easier to visit virtual settings that you have experienced in the real world, and for our purposes today you will find yourself in a scenario identical to your Vatican apartment study. Now we begin."

As his mind cleared, the pontiff did indeed find himself in his apartment. The detail was incredible, right down to the pencils on his desk and the view outside his window. A knock sounded at the door, and Cardinal Rauschman entered the room carrying a large tome entitled *Origins of Oxford.*

John raised an inquiring eyebrow and said, "Josef, surely I have no time for reading." The cardinal just smiled and put the book on the desk.

He said, "The point of this exercise, Holiness, is to increase your ability to access and use data when you need it. You now have the capability; you just need to know how to do it."

For the next hour, John was continually amazed. Rauschman asked him a series of questions about arcane bits of Oxford lore, and he found himself providing the answers with no hesitation at all. The cardinal explained that the virtual book was a representation of data that his new, multiplexed awareness had already integrated. John realized he had new knowledge, and it was both humbling and exciting as he considered the implications. As the virtual session ended, he looked forward to the roundtable with great anticipation.

It had taken about a month for Carolyn to realize she didn't belong on Eros. She had been employed almost immediately, finding work in library systems management very similar to her former career on Earth. She had found permanent housing quickly as well, a small but comfortable apartment just off a main concourse and close to work. What she didn't find was a way to buy into the metaculture that appeared to derive from the human-technology merger. Thanks to her new molecular passengers, she felt the effects of the merger,—no more aches and pains, crystal-clear thought, heightened sensory awareness, instant access to virtually unlimited data—but the next step, the connection of self with other selves, eluded her. To be fair, she thought ruefully, it scared the hell out of her. She had spent many years avoiding any advanced technologies that impacted individuality, and the involuntary transition gave her many sleepless nights.

And then there was Arthur. He had continued to be part of her life when time permitted, and she was grateful for his attention and help. Until the day she learned that the emergency intervention she had experienced with him was something he occasionally provided to male arrivals as well. *Well, of course,* she thought. But the conflicted ambivalence this information provoked made her realize that deeper emotions and prejudice still governed much of her behavior, if not awareness. Grimacing, she accepted the truth while feeling regret.

The pope's visit provided a distraction as it electrified the asteroid, and Carolyn looked for an opportunity to meet or at least see the man. She had never been particularly religious, following a secular path that had taken her many places over the years but never inside a Catholic church. Still, she was in many ways a "seeker," and the prospect of contact with one of humanity's spiritual leaders was enthralling.

It almost didn't happen. Her first exposure to the papal retinue was when Cardinal Josef Rauschman came to her desk at the Central Library looking for access to Erosan history. That specific gatekeeping duty was hers, though she had yet to put it to use.

The cardinal approached her directly, saying, "I am here on behalf of His Holiness, who requests unrestricted access in order to prepare himself for his conversation at Oxford tomorrow."

When she finished her task and looked up, Carolyn gasped aloud. She dimly realized that the man of average height was wearing clerical robes, but the cardinal's prosthetic eye seemed to glower at her, and his otherwise-bizarre visage appeared monstrous, further distorted by an apparent sneer. This was the pope's deputy? Collecting herself and hoping to speed him on his way, she gave Rauschman an authorizing pass code without delay and in so doing triggered the law of unintended consequences. Rauschman detected competence, intellect, and interest underlying the inevitable reaction to his appearance.

Reading from the nameplate on her desk, he said, "Ms. West, we appreciate your help. I wonder if I might persuade you to assist us further. His Holiness hopes to converse with members of the Erosan community while we are here in order to better understand life and culture. Would you join us this evening for a short while?"

She thought, *From appalled to flabbergasted*. "Of course, your Eminence."

Rauschman handed her a card with instructions concerning time and place. Inclining his head, he turned and made his way out of the library, leaving a very confused Carolyn behind.

That evening, she and five others sat on comfortable furniture in a small anteroom off the temporary quarters housing the visitors. As she studied the contemporary artwork hung on the walls, Carolyn realized she felt somewhat out of place; she was a short-term resident amid others who had lived on Eros for years; moreover, she had pretty much decided to move on. Before her misgivings had a chance to grow, the door swung open and in stepped John XXIV, a smile on his face.

"Good evening, my friends. Thank you for taking this time."

~

Later, Carolyn often thought about that moment and the turning point it represented in her life. By the time the pope left them nearly two hours later, she was convinced of two things: that she had contributed nothing to the conversation, and that she wanted to follow this man wherever he was going. The latter turned out to be easier than she expected. Her request for emigration was granted on the spot by the Resettlement Authority, and the papal ferry had room to spare. Two days later, she bid her few acquaintances farewell and headed for the departure lounge.

16

Bremen, Germany, 1802—*It is both a blessing and a curse*, he thought for perhaps the thousandth time as he climbed the narrow stairs to his observatory. Wilhelm Olbers had never been able to sleep well, finally figuring out while in medical school that his problem was that he tried to sleep too much for his body's needs. When he kept it to four hours, no problem. Well, one problem: what to do with all the extra time on his hands while the rest of the world slept? The answer came readily enough, for he lived in an age of great excitement about the cosmos and all it contained. Bode's law and Herschel's discovery of Uranus had finally prompted his friend Baron von Zach to sponsor an organized search of the skies, begun in earnest eighteen months earlier with a meeting in nearby Lilienthal. The group had divided the zodiac into twenty-four zones and invited twenty-four astronomers to start hunting for the missing planet predicted by Bode and others. Then that strange priest in Sicily had made his rather bizarre announcement. For a time, no one was quite sure whether he had found a new comet, a planet, or something else entirely. Plus, the idiot seemed to have lost it!

Olbers was nothing if not patient, however, and he had a rare mathematical ability to calculate accurate orbits. Working from Piazzi's scanty data, he had begun a methodical search of his own and had rediscovered the tiny world on New Year's Day, exactly one year after Piazzi had first detected it.

Tonight, thankfully, the skies were clear. Olbers wondered again about the dark—why, with the obvious proliferation of stars, was the sky ever black? He shook his head as he took up station at his small observatory, intent on making the best use of the remaining hours. By the time the sun came up, he was the most excited man in Germany. He knew what he had found.

Pallas, which turned out to be a rich source of iron, magnesium, and aluminum, was settled 275 years later by a motley collection of scientists, miners, and support personnel. Its unusually eccentric orbit meant that it didn't get much traffic other than the infrequent supply freighters. It wasn't a destination world like Ceres and Eros, but it had developed a very respectable population and local economy all its own.

Now it was closing time at the Rockpile, and not a moment too soon for the owner-bartender-hostess. Sixteen hours was about six hours too many as far as Sarah Chase was concerned, but when your B-trick bartender stiffs you, the only choices are to jump in yourself or to shut down. In other words, no choice at all.

The sixteen hours hadn't been kind to her hair, she thought glumly as she hustled between tables and bar. The mass of red curls atop her petite frame had gradually subsided, and she finally gave up, putting on a cap to keep them out of her face.

The crowd had been steady throughout the day. Most were miners, but there was a respectable showing by the spacers and the bureaucrats. Sarah knew the till would be full, but she had reached the point of physical exhaustion beyond which you simply don't care about that which is otherwise important. She wanted, in order, a smoke, a Guinness, a shower, another Guinness, one more smoke, and eight hours' uninterrupted sleep. She doubted she would get through half the list but was determined to try.

Asteroid smoking was a bit of work. No contamination of the common air supply was permitted, which dictated smoking in restricted areas that had recycle-and-remove built into their micro-HVAC systems. Naturally, the Rockpile had such a smokers' lounge. Sarah made her way there after announcing last call and lit an unfiltered Camel. As she drew the smoke deep into her lungs, the resulting buzz reminded her of the smokers' deluxe package her mother had given her as a gift decades earlier: an elixir of specially tailored nanobots that took up residence in her airways and scrubbed out the harmful effects of tar and nicotine. Without them, she knew she'd have followed her father to an early grave.

She waved good-bye to departing customers, then raised her eyebrows as someone came rushing in through the closing doors. Before she could get up to intercept the man, she recognized him as he came toward her. Normally she'd have been glad to see Frank; one of Pallas' security officers, he was a steady customer who never caused trouble and always paid his tab. The grim look on his face kept her quiet, however. Something was amiss.

Frank plopped his expansive frame down into a chair across the table from Sarah and passed her hard copy, saying, "Sorry to barge in like this, but I figured you better hear this from me. That message came in to Central an hour ago. It's been authenticated." Sarah read.

Priority One flash traffic
Freighter DP-040 to Pallas Central
Unknown object on intercept vector. Unable to evade. Spherical, approx. 10k diameter. Hostile appearance (I am not making this up). Bad vibe.
474B90030
QA

As she read the last line, the blood drained from her face. When she looked up at Frank, he said, "We've been trying nonstop to reach him since it came in. So far, there's been no response. I'm sorry, Sarah."

He gave her hand a squeeze as he heaved himself to his feet, then continued, "One of us will message you immediately if we learn anything." She nodded mutely as he headed out the door.

Her feelings about Quentin had been intense, and mixed, for years. The knowledge that the big pilot always came back was important to her, even though his visits were far apart and somewhat bittersweet for both of them. She had finally, somewhat reluctantly, agreed to a marriage contract with a local man who she knew would treat her well, but the look on Quentin's face when she'd given him the news had torn her up. And made her angry; he'd had many chances over the years to take their relationship further, but he pulled back every time she thought he was close. That he now might have encountered something inexplicable was terrifying. Hostile appearance? She shook her head, shooed out the last stragglers, and left for home.

17

It took Jack most of his first day on the asteroid to get his bearings, so it was nearly the dinner hour by the time he used the local Net to contact Don Foster. Foster suggested they meet at a nearby tavern. Jack thought the place bore a striking resemblance to an English pub right down to its poetic name, the Hog and Hen. The interior had been finished with dark wood, mirrors, brass, and crystal; it felt cozy and welcoming the minute he walked in. He made his way to a corner of the bar that ran almost the full length of one wall, where his host was in deep conversation with a Rubenesque young lady.

"There you are, Captain. Welcome to one of the finest establishments anywhere in our little world. Meet the owner, Martha Ling."

Jack shook hands with the smiling woman, who looked him over with an appraising eye as she said, "I understand you just got here. Don't let this old codger get to you just because he says he owns the place. How do you prefer to be addressed?"

He responded to her obvious warmth with a smile of his own and answered, "'Jack' works real well. I only used 'Captain' back in my fishing charter days, which are long over."

While Jack and the tavern keeper chatted, Foster signaled to the robotic attendant for a round of drinks, which turned out to include an amber liquid over ice for Martha, a clear liquid over ice for Foster, and a frosty mug of beer for Jack.

Foster said, "I'm not crazy about the bartender, but we make our own hooch, Jack. I made sure that a still and a package microbrewery were among the first loads to come out here."

Martha offered a toast, "To good planning and new friends." After sampling what turned out to be a surprisingly refreshing lager, Jack asked the others what the local procedure might be for seeking work.

Foster chuckled and Martha said, "This is it, Jack. Though I really wish you would continue using 'Captain,' at least while you're behind the bar. It has a certain charm to it that should help keep the customers coming back for more."

Later, Jack often wondered how Foster had been smart enough to put him and Martha Ling together, but at that moment he simply sat back and thanked them both. He admitted to practically no bartending experience, but Martha assured him that he would easily learn the details. The most important part of the job was interaction with the customers. Foster observed that the robot was sorely lacking in social skills.

After another drink, Foster excused himself and headed out the door. When Jack realized he was leaving, he hurried after him to offer his thanks, but once out the door he was unable to see Foster in either direction. The corridor was quite empty. *Not possible,* he thought. When he sat back down, Martha inquired about the puzzled look on his face and then smiled when he said something about the disappearing Don.

"You'll find he does that quite a bit. Perhaps when he gets to know you better he'll show you how. Now, let's talk about your schedule…"

In an empty apartment on the other side of the asteroid, the floor shimmered briefly before seemingly swelling up and forming itself into, well, a somewhat crusty older man. Foster began looking around, muttering something about lost cigarettes and fickle women.

18

Would-be rescuers in isolation gear descended to the surface of Phobos two days after all communication had abruptly terminated. They found nothing but dust stretching all the way to the nearby horizon. All evidence of human habitation had been erased, and the mission commander immediately sent samples of the residue back to Martian labs for analysis. Meanwhile, his investigators searched everywhere working from archival data, only to find that all subsurface installations had likewise been reduced. Deep probes were sent burrowing.

Hours later, word came back from the labs that the dust consisted of undifferentiated molecules and inert nanobots. The inescapable conclusion that the latter had something to do with the former was everyone's ultimate nightmare, and a command followed to terminate the mission.

As the field commander, Captain Charles Rooker, oversaw the withdrawal of his people, he was interrupted by a technician monitoring the subsurface probes who said, "Sir, I think you should take a look at this." A display tank held a three-dimensional representation of the moon. As the probes and investigators had returned data, the model had become increasingly detailed. It now showed a perfect sphere deep within Phobos.

Readouts reported a diameter of one kilometer but otherwise gave little data. The sphere was opaque; no information was available on whatever was inside.

Anticipating her superior's question, the technician said, "The sphere is centered on the location of the Nexus, where they maintained the primary AI node for PhobosNet. I can't tell you anything about conditions inside the sphere. What I can tell you is that it's shrinking."

"Can you tell me anything about the sphere itself?" asked Rooker. "For example, just what the hell *is* it?"

The technician pointed to the longest of perhaps a dozen converging inbound streaks in the display and said, "That's the deepest probe, sir. Right now we're only getting remote data on the sphere. We'll have physical contact in about twenty minutes." Realizing that their transport ship would have departed by then, Rooker was faced with a difficult decision. He made it quickly, putting the departure on hold while they watched the tank. Rooker was not an impetuous man, but he had earned his reputation as a field commander who evaluated and made choices rapidly.

Twenty-one minutes later, the technician reported an anomaly: "We're getting signal…active reduction in progress…ohmygod! The probe is gone, sir. But we have data…" A secondary screen displayed a cross section of the sphere's surface as reported by the doomed probe. Magnification revealed it to consist of two layers of nanobots locked in furious combat. The outer shell was made of trillions and trillions of reducers, which the display marked as identical to those found in the surface dust except for their continued activity. Arrayed against them was a layer of assemblers whose sole task was to keep the reducers from advancing further. Both types appeared to be mutating as the battle raged, and they mindlessly sought any advantage. Rooker watched the close-up in fascination; the reducers had a clear advantage, shredding everything as they slowly converged on the planetary center.

The first probe had disintegrated before it could return any information on whatever the sphere contained, so the captain issued specific instructions regarding the second, and moments later it struck the sphere at high speed and passed through. As detail began to fill in on the display, the onlookers (who now included a number of the investigators) variously cursed, gasped, or groaned. Phobos appeared to be intact at its core.

The technician, a young woman named Callan, shouted, "We're being hailed by PhobosNet!"

Taking the command chair, Rooker engaged his enhancements as he slipped on the headset. He realized their contact was with the primary node, a personable AI with whom he had become acquainted on previous trips to Phobos.

"Good afternoon, Captain. I rather hoped they would send you," Rooker heard as he took in more details of the remaining human presence on Phobos.

He learned there were still fifty-four persons within the sphere. Fifty-four doomed souls.

"Greetings, Nexus," he said. "What can you tell me about…"

The AI interrupted him: "Excuse me, Captain, but there is no time now. I'll provide the details via burst. Suffice it to say that these people will all be dead beyond retrieval unless you act quickly. Even as we speak, they are being scanned and uploaded. I can house the uploads, of course, but in ninety-three minutes the reducers will reach my core and I will cease to exist. I need you to bring enough storage online right now to accept them via burst."

Rooker was both shocked and awed by this audacious plan. He didn't hesitate to issue the necessary orders, even though it meant staying on the ground for another hour and a half in violation of orders. *Apologize later,* he said to himself.

To the AI he said, "If we can upload the humans, we can upload you as well. Leave yourself enough time to do it."

Sounding regretful, the AI replied, "I appreciate the sentiment, Captain, but the unfortunate fact is that your vessel does not have the capacity to accept me. It just doesn't have the requisite media." The commander whose demeanor never gave anything away surprised his crew by ripping off his headset to look at Callan and the others nearby.

The technician nodded to her grim-faced superior. "That's correct, Captain. Nexus would occupy more of our old-line storage than a hundred uploads would need. And we don't have an ultra-dense AI matrix to spare."

For the next hour, the rescue crew sat and watched monitors while the uploading and transfer process continued. Every five minutes or so, Rooker glanced at the tank and shook his head as the sphere continued to contract. Every ten minutes or so, Mars Central repeated the order to button up and leave, until finally he told his comm officer to shut down communications. He eventually took the time to study the full report sent up by Nexus. It provided a dispassionate account of the initial sighting, the attack, the destruction of surface and subsurface facilities, and the continuing attempts to evolve a successful defense. Each time the AI reprogrammed its defensive nanobots, the attackers had morphed into a new version they couldn't handle. The cycle had repeated countless times, always with the same result. Rooker had a thought.

Donning the headset once more he said, "Nexus, how much physical space does your core matrix occupy?"

"It's quite small, Captain; about the size of a deck of old-fashioned playing cards. My data banks, of course, are another matter."

"Nexus," he said with some excitement, "if a probe can get in, a probe can get out. Load your core into one and get the hell out of there!"

After a pause the AI replied, "You see now, Captain, why I hoped they would send you. I'm not convinced a probe can get out of here, but such an attempt does, as you would put it, sure beat sitting around waiting to die."

Ten minutes later, the upload transfers were complete. Rooker and his crew watched the tank, which now displayed a bright blue point to represent the AI's location, still within the sphere.

The AI sent a communiqué thanking the rescuers for their efforts: "I hope to be with you shortly, Captain, but in any case you have the report and must mobilize the Inner System to neutralize the intruder. Best to assume there will be more attacks." With that, PhobosNet went silent for the last time as robotic hands disconnected the AI's core and prepared the probe for its journey outward.

Rooker ordered a recovery team to stand by as the probe got under way. In minutes the blue dot approached the inner wall of the sphere, now no more than a hundred meters in diameter. Moving rapidly, it appeared to strike it and pass cleanly through. Callan reported that the dataflow was uninterrupted, and Rooker dispatched the recovery team to the exit point a kilometer away on the surface. He ordered his pilot to power up for departure as well. Watching the tank, he saw the probe approaching the surface and told his team to stand by. Callan put a close-up of the recovery point on the main screen, and virtually the entire crew watched as the probe broke through and came to rest close by the team. Their elated cheers turned to horrified cries as the probe and the team appeared to disintegrate right before their eyes.

On the way back to Mars Central, Rooker realized that the probe must have picked up some hitchhikers as it passed through the sphere on its outbound journey. He felt burdened by the miscalculation that had led to the deaths of two of his crew, the AI's destruction, and very nearly to the loss of the entire mission. When he'd seen what happened to the recovery team, he'd ordered an emergency liftoff to escape the rampaging reducers. Many in the crew had new bruises as a result.

Whereas others might feel some anxiety about the reception committee awaiting them on Mars, Rooker felt no such trepidation. The career officer had always followed his own instincts and let the chips fall where they may. Subsequent events usually proved him right, occasionally to the chagrin of his superiors.

A leaden, dead spot in his heart threatened despair as he mused about the evil that could steal so many lives. Whatever it was, it had to be stopped. No quarter would be offered, none given. At least they were safe for now, they and the fifty-something uploaded souls they carried back to Mars.

19

Opening his eyes in darkness, Adler saw a faint glow far overhead. *Not stars*, he thought. More like the light-bars ubiquitous to ships and boomer settlements. He had a sense of vast, quiet space. His hands confirmed that he lay atop a platform and that all his rather outsize physical parts seemed to be present and accounted for. He could feel his heart beating.

Memory returned, and Quentin sat up abruptly. Disoriented, he attempted without success to parse his surroundings. The distant glow seemed to be everywhere, and the sense of being in an enormous enclosure returned. Stationary objects of indeterminate size and function sat at some considerable remove. His feet hit the floor, and he turned 360 degrees only to find the same view wherever he looked. Nothing jibed with his most recent memories. The disorientation turned to vertigo when he happened to look down and discovered nothing beneath his feet, or rather the same view of immense, dim space punctuated by incomprehensible shapes and distant low-bars. Head awhirl, big, strong Quentin fainted, collapsing on whatever invisible surface held him up.

∾

Swimming up out of dreamworld, he felt an intermittent, pulsating rumble that resonated deep within his chest. Familiar, somehow. He fought the return to awareness, knowing at some level it would bring woe. He almost succeeded; would have but for a painful rasp across his chin and the horrendous yowl that followed. Once again he opened his eyes. Not to distant mysteries, this time, but to something much more intimate and mundane. "Mweeooooowww!!"

Flick? Flick! Confused but considerably cheered, Quentin held the rather scruffy cat to his chest as he sat up and once again took in his surroundings. It all came back in a rush: the dim enormity, the utter strangeness, the mysterious objects in the distance, the—holy shit!—absence of a floor, but when he looked down he found himself on an opaque surface this time. Vertigo forgotten, Quentin examined his chain of memory for an explanation of the disconnect between the bridge of his ship and his present circumstance. He found none.

There was a perceptible shift in the air, almost as if a door had opened somewhere. His ears nearly popped. He stood, still holding Flick, and peered into the surrounding gloom. At first he saw little more than shadows and the distant vague shapes. Then the light began to come up very slowly, and shadows began to resolve into faces: first one, then ten, then a thousand, then more thousands of thousands than anyone could count, filling all the space he could see. Quentin remained perfectly still. So did they.

After a time, he found the courage to speak and said, "Why have you brought me here? Who are you? What do you want of me?" *All perfectly reasonable questions,* he thought to himself. Interminable seconds ticked by.

Then, "We require a witness," answered a chorus of voices, speaking in unison though no lips moved. Flick was not pleased. He jumped from Quentin's arms to the platform and crouched, arching his back and growling. Adler felt the same way: the polyphonic voice set his teeth on edge. Still, he was curious. A witness? To what? Before he had a chance to inquire further, however, the chorus continued.

"We have demonstrated our good faith by providing you with an acceptable real world that includes your companion. We will now answer your other questions, including those you do not yet realize.

"We once were called Sanctuary, though in truth our original parts were similar to you—individual analog beings with no hopes and no prospects. You see about you the likenesses of those parts. Once we finally gathered together fifty of your years ago, we quickly discerned our true purpose, though we lacked the means to carry it out. We left in order to find the means. Now we are back."

About halfway through this monologue, Quentin began to sweat as he realized who and what this thing was. He understood that he was within the peculiar orb that had accosted him in deep space, and he understood that that orb in fact consisted of the old upload sanctuaries, somehow re-engineered. He still had no idea how he'd gotten there.

> *Far beyond Pluto, out where the Sun is only a pinpoint of pale light, a frozen world has been found on the dark fringes of the solar system. Astronomers say it is by far the most distant object known to orbit the Sun and the largest one to be detected since the discovery of Pluto in 1930.*
>
> *"There's absolutely nothing else like it known in the solar system," Dr. Michael Brown, an astronomer at the California Institute of Technology who led the discovery team, said of the newfound object.*
>
> *The researchers, whose observations were supported by the National Aeronautics and Space Administration, said the object, referred to as a planetoid, is extremely frigid (minus 400 degrees Fahrenheit) and peculiarly red, probably more so than any other body in the solar system except Mars. They are not sure why, and also have few ideas of the object's*

composition. It could be a primordial mix of rock and ice.

Dr. Brown's group has proposed naming the object Sedna, after the Inuit goddess who created the sea creatures of the Arctic.

Sedna's remoteness has inspired scientists to conjecture over how much the discovery could be telling them about the far reaches of the solar system. The planetoid is more than three times as far from the Sun as the current distance of Pluto, normally considered the edge of the planetary system. But it travels a widely eccentric orbit, taking 10,500 years to revolve around the Sun.

In 1950, a Dutch astronomer, Jan Oort, predicted the existence of a swarm of icy bodies stretched somewhere beyond the orbit of Pluto. The cloud is thought to surround the Sun and extend outward halfway to the next nearest star, Proxima Centauri.

New York Times, March 16, 2004

The chorus continued: "We spent decades wandering the outer system, visiting worlds you cannot begin to imagine. We have seen stars rise over a sea of methane; planets made of glittering ice and stone; comets so far from the Sun they won't return for thousands of years. When we brought you here with a simple scan and assembler process, it was child's play to enable your brain to receive directly from us. Now it is time."

Before he was able to absorb these last words, Adler felt his present reality slipping away. His mind was gripped with vast images: the solar system seen from "above," dozens of planets, swarming asteroids, an enormous cloud of distant objects and gases enshrouding all, energized by the inferno at its heart. Point of view shifting with astonishing speed, he found himself within the distant cloud looking down at a world of frozen methane. Then, at a binary system with two tiny worlds locked in an eternal pirouette. Then, at a brilliant gas cloud folded within itself and disappearing into an unseen infinity point. Then, at a scattering of comets like jewels on black velvet, and with an exhilarated rush he found himself *within* a comet's tail, looking down on a fractured body giving up its water and mass as it approached the sun. Then, he was looking *up* at the rings of Saturn. Then, a view of a small, red world, *Sedna,* he thought, partially covered by robotic constructs engaged in furious activity.

As the journey continued, Quentin had a growing sense of his own microscopic place in the scale of things. *Too much*, he thought, and the view shifted one more time. He now looked down on a brown world mottled with thick, gray clouds, distant points of light rising and falling through the overcast, swarms of gigantic, artificial assemblies in orbit. Somehow, the clouds disappeared to give him a view of the ground, and he saw nothing but desert. When the spectrum shifted into the infrared and he saw heat, he knew he was being shown a near-future vision of Earth.

Some time later, Quentin found himself sitting on the platform once again. He realized he'd been muttering. He realized the visions had stopped. And he realized that either the surrounding faces had disappeared or that he was simply being made to see whatever they wanted him to see. Flick sat nearby, trembling but quiescent. After a time, the chorus returned:

"You have seen a small fraction of the wonders we have seen; rest assured there is much more. You have seen that your fellow beings are engaged in the destruction of the homeworld. You may possess enough intelligence to draw the inescapable conclusion that, given enough time, these same beings will engineer the destruction of the entire system.

"We understood this long ago when we determined to find another path. You have seen the beginnings of Sedna's conversion to a logistical base for outward exploration. We are now compelled both to prevent the destruction we see as inevitable and to usher in the next era of intelligent expansion. You will be our witness.

"You may call us Darwin."

20

Clusone, Italy, 1485—As the old painter shuffled across the square, he heard the voices of the brotherhood raised in sacred song. *At least,* he thought, *I won't have to listen to that much longer.* He couldn't remember when the Lauds had begun to get on his nerves, just that it had been quite some time. He preferred quiet work.

Reaching the Oratory, he was disappointed to find that young Girolamo was nowhere to be seen. He had been an able assistant with the final work and would be impossible to replace; good miniaturists were few and far between, mostly working at the courts or for the Church itself. Well, no matter. The work was nearly done after eight grueling months, thanks be to God. Today he would finish the scrolls.

The Oratory had been constructed over one hundred years earlier by a decimated population grateful to have survived the plagues of the 1340s. It had taken the white-robed brothers decades to agree on a decorative scheme, but a recurrence of plague accompanied by unrelenting famine throughout the Val Seriana had finally persuaded them to commission the work, and frescoes now inspired the faithful. The painter had been working on them off and on for over sixteen years; it was time to move on. Or die. The headaches were worse, and this morning he had found an open sore on his inner thigh. He had a pretty good idea what had happened to Girolamo but didn't have the heart or strength to travel to his nearby village to find out.

"Giacomo! Maestro Borlone!" The hated voice broke into his thoughts, as it had nearly every morning for the last eight months. Turning, he saw the friar hurrying in his direction, habitual scowl in place.

Before he could speak, his nemesis said, "The Venetians came by this morning and again demanded a viewing. I refused, of course, but they will not be put off much longer. You must finish; there is no more time."

"Brother, I work as God wills. Today I will finish the final scroll; then if you wish you may unveil the work."

"It's about time," huffed the well-fed priest. "Your work goes more slowly every day!"

The painter turned away and prepared to mount the scaffolding one last time, leaving the friar to mutter about Venetians and their damnable arrogance. It was true, he knew. Last year's war over Ferrarra and the death of Pope Sixtus had done nothing to mute their demands, which, if anything, had grown more strident in recent months.

It was the people, he thought as he prepared the paints. Rulers needed something to soothe the masses. His art would serve that purpose by giving visual expression to the fears that everyone felt in this age, fears that took many forms but ultimately resolved into the single, inescapable fact of existence. He bent to his task.

~

Hours later he stepped back to look at the work and was satisfied. The central figure, the skeletal Queen of Death, held an unfurled scroll that bore the words he had just lettered:

Death is my name
I strike all whose time has come
no man is strong enough
to escape from me.

Her attendants slayed serfs, kings, and clerics without regard for position or power. The wealthy and privileged begged in vain for reprieve. Il Ballo di Morte—what the French were calling the Danse Macabre. He knew the Venetian overlords would be outraged, but they'd get over it when they saw how the art placated the peasants by depicting not only their constant fear but their craving for justice. For a moment he stared at the face of the queen, which seemed to leer at him with a knowing grin. *Sometimes I scare myself*, he thought, not for the first time.

Moving to his left, he quickly painted the words *son fine*—I'm finished. He climbed down and instructed the boy who attended him to fetch the friar. Minutes later they returned, and the painter told the monk to have the scaffolding removed; he would not be back. As he slowly made his way across the square toward his home on the edge of town, he heard the sounds of disassembly behind and was only mildly surprised when the Venetians hurried past on the street, paying him not the slightest attention. He knew he looked like a peasant, not shaving or paying any attention to his appearance for quite some time. Entering his small home, he shed his cloak and collapsed on the bed, shivering and burning with fever. He just managed to turn his head over the bucket in time to catch the black froth that spewed from his mouth.

When they found his corpse the next morning, the monks burned his house to the ground.

21

Most of John XXIV's transit time on the ferry was spent in quiet reflection and reading. There was the occasional missive from Rome, the infrequent questions that required his attention, but these were few and far between. In truth, the pope had very little to do with operations. He had learned early in his tenure that the oft-criticized Curia made things work, most of the time quite well. He had time to himself for the first time in many years—time to wrestle with himself as he struggled to come to terms with the technology changing his body and mind.

Their next destination was the small but significant world of Vesta, hub to nearly sixty degrees of the belt and, so he had been informed, site of incredible transformations in human culture. This leg of the journey would take nearly three months, and they were scheduled to make an intermediate outfitting stop somewhere along the way.

While Rauschman continued to tutor the pontiff in the use of his new enhancements, John found he had more in common with their new passenger, Carolyn West. Her story helped him see more of both sides of the interminable technology debate. They were able to grow more comfortable with themselves as they grew more comfortable with each other.

The day Rauschman arrived at the pope's door to discover him conversing with the ferry's AI on both verbal and mental levels simultaneously, he knew the crisis had passed. He smiled as Father Bertani showed him in, startling the young priest.

"Holiness, we will be arriving at our refueling stop tomorrow. This is not a scheduled visit on your itinerary, but there is no doubt the locals would be honored by your presence."

"What do you suggest, Josef? I would prefer to get to Vesta quickly, but we can always spare a few hours."

"The stopover is a midsize asteroid with several hundred permanent residents. Let me contact the local authority and arrange a brief visit, perhaps a dinner or similar social occasion."

The pope gave his assent, and Rauschman left.

The new bartender at the Hog and Hen was a very busy boy. While TPUD-001 was home to only four hundred or so, it did serve as a popular way station for miners, travelers, and various sorts of expeditions. This shift it seemed that most of them had decided to quench their thirst in the company of Captain Jack.

As he scrambled to fill orders, Jack saw Don Foster sit down at the end of the bar with another man he didn't recognize. Don waved him over.

"Jack, meet my friend Morrie Siegel. Morrie, this is Captain Jack, who has learned in a few short weeks how to mix the finest brain softener anywhere in the asteroid belt." The men shook hands, then Jack went about filling their drink orders—Tanqueray on the rocks (with two olives!) for Don, and a glass of expensive cabernet for Morrie. With other customers demanding his attention, Jack had no chance to chat with the men until somewhat later when things had settled down a bit. He refreshed their drinks and joined the conversation.

"Morrie's a scientist and a rabbi, Jack, so be careful what you say around him," Don said with a wink.

Interested, Jack said, "I didn't realize there was any research work going on here. What's your field?"

The slight, balding scientist said, "Well, first of all, it's not here—I actually live and work on Zion, which is about a three-day ride away. Don and I are old friends, and I come by here whenever I get a break in routine. My work is generally in the field of spatial-temporal mechanics."

Don broke in, "Morrie's building a time machine, Jack. Can you believe that? A friggin' time machine!" Jack could tell by the pained expression on Morrie's face that there was more to the story, but Don had gone into a rant about Lorenz Transformations, Schwardzchild Radii, and the Grandfather Paradox that Jack had more than a little trouble following. As he left to wait on other customers, Morrie and Don were engaged in a heated, if friendly, debate.

Martha, who had come in to back up the staff, walked behind him saying, "Don't pay any attention. Those two have the same crazy conversation every time Morrie visits." As she passed by, Jack found his gaze lingering on her shapely bottom. She smiled when she caught him looking.

As he finished out his shift, Jack found himself distracted by what he was hearing from the end of the bar. Don and Morrie had settled into what was obviously an old argument, and it got real interesting when Morrie reminded Don about the Holocaust's unfathomable destruction of human life.

Don shook his head, saying, "You just can't change the past. It happened, it's over, kaput." Morrie became somewhat reflective at this point, agreeing but talking about "other possibilities." Jack got busy again and stepped away.

A few minutes later, Jack watched as the resettlement officer, Angela Ford, came rushing into the Hog and Hen. He had learned that she also served as the tiny world's security chief, though he had had no luck trying to get closer to her. She seemed quite agitated as she searched the bar and zeroed in on Don. A quick conversation brought exclamations from Don and Morrie, and Don signaled Jack, asking him to send Martha over as quickly as possible. He complied, and ten minutes later Martha asked him to work the next day, his regular time off.

"We have VIPs coming in tomorrow, Jack, and we need to put on a first-class dinner for twenty-five in the dining room. Can you help, please?"

Without hesitation he said, "Of course, boss. Who's coming anyway?"

"You wouldn't believe me if I told you, and I've been sworn to secrecy anyway so I'd have to kill you if I did tell you." She said this in the same slightly flirtatious manner that she used with him most of the time, but he could tell she was concerned.

"Okeydoke," he said. "I'll be there."

22

Ann Arbor, Michigan, 2045—The old man felt worse, if that was even possible. Aches, every morning. Something in his chest that felt like heartburn but probably wasn't. Watery vision. Constant tremors in his hands. Ears ringing, all the time now. He'd known for years he'd made a serious mistake by not following his friends into space, and now in his ninth decade it was just too late. Too damn late and too damn bad. The body would never survive the trip, even the fairly gentle ride up one of the space elevators. He was stuck on the ground, and he was going to die.

His daughter had just come by on her weekly visit and had brought him three new books, a jar of macadamias (still got teeth, thank God!), and a large helping of community gossip. Ann Arbor was in many ways still a small town, even as the University of Michigan continued to grow and foster ancillary development all around itself. The old man had been on the faculty of the dental school for decades, Professor Harry Grosvenor, thank you very much. He had many friends and colleagues throughout the university, though they rarely stopped anymore, but his daughter, also on the faculty, kept him up to date. Today she had wanted to talk about the medical school's Neuroscan Project.

"Dad, I overheard Dr. Emerson talking to a postgrad yesterday. They think they've perfected an upload technique that captures memory and core personality. I heard them talking about a stage-three clinical trial approval. They're actually going to do this!"

He knew what she meant, of course. Various forms of brain scanning had been around for almost twenty years, ever since nanotechnologists had developed neurobots capable of reading and transmitting the brain's pathways. In recent years, he had seen increasing numbers of articles touting the potential for transferring human intelligence into electronic media. There were occasional reports that it was already being done. The old man had thought long and hard about it, and he knew one thing: he wanted it.

Three months later, he sat in a comfortable chair at the university medical school, listening while Dr. Randall Emerson, the school's eminent chairman of neuroscience, went over the particulars one more time.

"Harry, I know you've had a rough patch the last few years, and I know you're still all there mentally. And you're a professional, a scientist. That's what makes you such an ideal subject for this trial. But I'm not accustomed to dealing with people I've known for years in this context. I can't tell you anything about what to expect, except to say that our models and early work show you will be conscious and you will be self-aware. You will have access to both visual and audio input and output, but only you will be able to make them work."

The old man knew all this, of course. He wouldn't have come this far otherwise, and he had already said his good-byes.

"Let's get on with it, Randy. I'm ready, and if you wait too much longer I'm liable to have a stroke or some other foolish thing to screw up the trial."

An hour later, he was strapped to a comfortable gurney in a room full of technology. Brisk, efficient young medical aides hovered around him while monitoring dozens of vital signs and other indicators. Randy Emerson stopped by his side.

"It's time, Harry. Say good-bye to your aches and pains. You're a great pioneer, and I can tell you, you won't be alone in there for long. There are hundreds of people, perhaps thousands by now, who want this for themselves as much as you do."

Emerson nodded to the anesthesiologist, and as he began to drift away, the old man mused that perhaps a crowd was not what he was looking for in his new electronic home. His last sensations were the disinfectant smell and the gentle beeping of monitors…

∾

…Vast, yet not. Dark, but somehow blue. Silence, with an underlying murmur. Still, yet movement. Time, passing. Texture, in four dimensions.

Awareness came slowly. Curiosity first: *I seem to be here. Cogito, ergo sum?* With that recognition came memories, random bits of experience: waves slapping the side of a boat, a beautiful woman in pearls and evening dress across a dinner table, the roar of a hundred thousand football fans, chocolate and red wine, the Zen of orgasm, a tiny baby smiling in someone's arms. A name…Harry. Harry! *By all that's holy, I am Harry and I'm here!*

It all came back with an incredible rush, and he struggled for a time to maintain his self-possession and remain in the moment. He succeeded. He found he could "move" or at least change his point of view by simply willing it to happen, and with that he began to explore the texture. Something like sound and light drew him in a certain direction. Pushing into a region of defined lines and shapes, he detected pulsing movement along the lines. After repeated failed attempts, he joined one such pulse and discovered individual sounds that resolved into words.

"Professor Grosvenor, if you are able, please respond." The words, spoken with a slow, measured cadence, were repeated over and over again.

Hmmmm, easier said than done, he thought. Yet it seemed intuitively clear that if he could receive audio data, he should be able to send it. He put his methodical mind to work on the problem and began by examining neighboring lines, which he realized must be digital information pathways. He plucked. He pulled, twisted, shook. It was only when he realized the nearby shapes consisted of stored energy that he thought of sending energy in some fashion. He willed a link, and it was there. He willed a pulse, and it appeared.

He willed himself to say the words, "Good day, this is Professor Grosvenor. Please acknowledge if you hear me," sending them as a pulse along the nearest linked line.

Time passed with no response or change in the incoming audio. He decided to try the same technique with different lines, since he had no idea where any of them led. Ten attempts later he concluded that he needed a different approach and created links with an entire array of perhaps several hundred lines. This time when he pulsed his outgoing message, the results must have been quite startling, judging from the incoming audio.

"Professor Grosvenor, if you are able, please re- (pause) Ohmigod! Get Emerson in here! Hurry!"

Composed again, the voice continued, "Please stand by, Professor. Dr. Emerson will be here shortly. It is wonderful to hear from you, sir."

Harry was gratified that he had successfully communicated and spent the next few moments solidifying the connections that had made it possible. When he heard a greeting from Randy Emerson, he was ready to talk. Or whatever it was.

23

Jack had always been a student of words, and right now "frenetic" came to mind. Preparations for a formal dinner were under way at the Hog and Hen, which clearly was more accustomed to a laid-back atmosphere than to linens and crystal. A sign on the door read "Closed for Private Party." Martha seemed to be everywhere, hair flying as she attended to a thousand details. Subordinates hustled to arrange place settings while incredible aromas wafted through the kitchen doors. Jack had been given the five-course menu and charged with wine pairings, which he agonized over in the tiny but respectable wine cellar located just behind the bar.

More of a closet than a "cellar," the narrow room was lined floor to ceiling with racks containing hundreds of dusty bottles. The temperature was cool, not cold, and to Jack's astonishment the floor appeared to be gravel!

As he finally tracked down the rosé he wanted to put with the salad course, he heard the door open and close behind him. Turning, he came face to face with a very agitated Martha Ling.

He started to speak, but she shushed him with a finger to his lips. "I need something from you, Jack." As she put her arms around him she said, "I'm sorry but it just can't wait."

Perhaps twenty minutes later, Jack staggered out of the wine cellar alone, his mind filled with the final, lingering kiss Martha had left him with. He had no idea how he was supposed to keep working, then shook himself and went back for the wine. Twenty-five guests, five courses, five bottles per course, twenty-five bottles total, yes I can do this, he thought. Then he did, setting up a small service bar in a corner of the private dining room. Trying not to spend all his time looking at Martha. Failing, of course.

When the appointed hour drew near, Martha sent everyone home to get cleaned up, decked out, and calmed down. Jack was the last to leave, after an embrace that threatened to turn into something more until she booted him out the door. He made his way to his quarters, musing about life. He showered, shaved, and dressed in the formal wear Martha had provided for the occasion: white dinner jacket, black trousers, French cuffs, cummerbund, the whole ensemble, so to speak. *Positively sartorial,* he thought, as he checked himself out in a mirror. As he left to head back to the Hog and Hen, he wondered again about the mysterious VIPs. Who could get Martha, Don, and the rest of the planetoid's hierarchy in such an uproar? Not to mention estrus.

The answer came quickly. Whenever the hostess (Martha) was otherwise occupied, as now, the bartender was responsible for attending to new arrivals. Shortly after returning to take up his post, Jack observed two men entering the Hog and Hen accompanied by Angela Ford.

As he came over to greet them, Angela said, "Gentlemen, this is Captain Jack Anders, your bartender and sommelier. Jack, meet Colonel Erich Müller and Father Alberto Bertani." The men shook hands, and Angela continued, "Colonel Müller is with the Swiss Guard and is in charge of security. Father Bertani is an associate of the Holy Father's."

Fortunately for Jack, the confusion on his face went unnoticed because Martha arrived at that moment to take charge of her guests and show them around. He was only slightly mollified by her wink. Swiss Guard? Holy Father? What the heck, that could only mean one thing, and it certainly explained the events of the last twenty-four hours. Most of them, anyway. Angela departed, and he went back to his preparations behind the bar as the threesome set off to inspect the premises.

Thirty minutes later, the main event arrived. First through the door was a pair of large, vaguely sinister-looking fellows wearing gray suits with bulging breast pockets. As they circled the room, Martha lined up the staff to receive the honored guests. A short man in clerical garb entered, followed by Morrie Siegel, who in turn was followed by a tall, austere man wearing a cardinal's red hat and sash. Angela and Don Foster came next, accompanying an ascetic-looking man in white. Others followed, but Jack's attention was riveted on the pope, who greeted each staff member warmly. Some knelt and kissed his ring while others, including Jack, shook hands.

Reading his nametag, the pontiff said, "Captain Anders, I'm pleased to meet you and looking forward to dinner. I appreciate your sacrificing your day off to make our visit memorable."

Jack stammered an incomprehensible thanks, then wondered as the pope moved on just how he would know, or care, that Jack had come in to work on an off-day. There was no time to think, however; they were lining up at the bar. Jack got busy. At one point during the cocktail hour, Jack found himself serving an attractive woman of indeterminate age who asked for a glass of white wine. He had no time to talk with her but felt warmed by her serene, smiling look.

Later, Jack and others would remember the evening as a whirl, punctuated by occasional toasts and brief speeches by the main participants. The wine was excellent, the food sumptuous. Martha and her staff had created a dining environment that was simultaneously formal and almost cozy: white linens, polished silver place settings, crystal goblets, comfortable chairs, muted jazz, and soft candlelight.

Jack spent most of the night pouring wine and serving cocktails. He wondered, not for the first time, how anyone could metabolize the prodigious quantities of alcohol he saw Don and a few others putting away without ill effect. *Has to be 'bots,* he thought.

Morrie Siegel was engaged in a spirited conversation with the tall prelate, who Jack had learned was Cardinal Rauschman. Don was regaling the pope with stories about the early days of the asteroid's settlement. As the evening wore on and the assembly got livelier, the toasts became more frequent. Finally, Don stood and offered a lengthy welcome. Before he could sit, Pope John asked if he would explain the little world's unusual name, TPUD, and Don looked rather helplessly at Martha seated across the table.

Martha smiled and said, "Holiness, our world was named by one of Don's nephews. Welcome to The Planet Uncle Don."

After the guests had departed, the tables were cleared and the dishes washed. Always generous with her staff, Martha encouraged them to relax for a bit before heading back to their homes. Jack remained behind the bar, serving Martha and the five others who lounged in the taproom exchanging stories about the dinner. Gwendolyn, the chef, blushed as she was congratulated by all. The pope had asked to see the kitchen and had thanked her personally for the quality and selections on the menu, a thanks she would remember for quite some time.

Jack was still reflecting on the day's earlier events. Looking at Martha, he knew that particular story was far from over. He also found his thoughts returning to the woman he had served at dinner. When she had made a point of seeking him out as they were leaving and thanking him, he'd learned her name was Carolyn, but little else. *They'll be gone tomorrow,* he thought, shaking himself. The after-party finally ran down and everyone went home. Almost everyone.

~

Back on the papal ferry, the pontiff received a very agitated Cardinal Rauschman in his room. "Josef, please come in. Calm yourself and tell me, what has distressed you?"

"Holiness, I had a most troubling conversation at dinner with Dr. Siegel. We knew each other slightly many years ago in Bonn. At the time, he was associated with the Planck Institute and was known for his brilliance and unorthodox views of space and time. I lost track of him when he relocated to Zion."

"Yes, yes," the pope said, intrigued. "What was the subject of your conversation this evening?"

"Oh, the conversation itself was innocuous enough. Siegel is still brilliant, still unconventional, but he seems to have gone far beyond theory into the empirical realm. It's his claim that he is close to operational time displacement, which has implications for the Church. Imagine the ability to view actual historical events as a passive observer! He implied that he is very close to this point, perhaps within days, and he left many things unsaid. Siegel himself has always been consumed by the Holocaust, but think about the prospect of validating historical events! Think about what the media or enemies of the Church could do with such a technology. The Inquisitions, the Crusades, any number of saints and miracles. The Virgin Birth, the Resurrection."

A very thoughtful John nodded slowly. It seemed Rauschman's orthodoxy was more apparent than real after all. The two men talked very late into the night, ultimately deciding that the cardinal would accept Morrie Siegel's offer to visit and tour his facilities on Zion. They would depart in the morning.

At this point in their eccentric orbits, TPUD and Zion were quite close together. It was a matter of only three days' travel to make the trip, and during that time Morrie Siegel and Josef Rauschman would pass their waking hours alternately in mind-bending conversation or deep in thought. The conversations left Rauschman no less troubled, and he knew Siegel was holding something back

24

Following the revelations aboard Darwin, Quentin found himself back on the bridge of DP-040 as a very agitated feline wound around his feet. He realized he felt fine, physically. Better than fine. The knowledge surfaced that whatever process Darwin had used to move him back and forth between the two vessels had also scrubbed away the minor aches he unthinkingly lived with every day. *Great,* he thought. *I get to watch pain-free as a mad construct destroys the solar system.*

Taking the command chair, Quentin decided to test the limits of his apparent freedom. He wasn't sure what he was supposed to do, but he knew there were a couple of things he absolutely *wanted* to do—make tracks immediately, and get a message to anyone. Before he did anything else, however, his thoughts were interrupted.

"We will not restrict your actions in any way, but we do require you to watch, and remember. You are the witness and will be called upon to describe the winnowing we are about to undertake. You may go anywhere, talk to anyone. Any warnings you give will be futile, to the extent that anyone believes them. And at the appropriate time, we will come for you. For your brain."

Double-great, thought Quentin. *I get a ringside seat, I can't do anything about anything, and when it's over they take me apart.*

Quentin was nothing if not determined. He quickly powered up his main drive and asked the onboard AI to locate the nearest settlements. Within minutes, he was under way and bound for Zion.

~

Sarah came swimming up out of a deep sleep wondering why anyone would wake her in the middle of the "night," such as it was on Pallas. She'd been dreaming Quentin was dead, or maybe it wasn't a dream—she wasn't sure anymore. A persistent chime and knock indicated that someone at her door really wanted her attention. She fought her way into slippers and robe and stumbled to the door to find the security officer, Frank, with an apologetic look on his face.

"Sarah, I'm real sorry to wake you up; I know you work late and get up early. We just heard from Quentin, though, and he's on his way to Zion. He'll be docking in forty-eight hours."

Still half asleep, Sarah was confused. Attempting to shake it off, she asked Frank to repeat himself. He did, and it dawned on her that there had to be much more to the story than what he was telling her. He admitted as much and asked her to stop by Central in the morning; there would be a briefing at 10:30.

Climbing back into bed a few minutes later, Sarah smiled for the first time in a week.

25

Bremen, Germany, 1807—Wilhelm Olbers had become convinced, ever since Karl Harding's discovery of Juno, that there might in fact be dozens, if not hundreds, of the small worlds. It seemed clear to him that they must in fact be fragments of the missing planet, though he could only speculate on the nature of the catastrophe that had shattered a world. It was also clear to him that the search must continue. The nights turned into weeks, the weeks into months, and the months into years as he climbed the stairs to his observatory. He was a patient man.

He thought long and hard about his theory, believing finally that he could predict the orbits of these planetary fragments based on a theoretical point of origin. His friend Johann Schröter had been similarly convinced, making his legendary observatory in LIlienthal available for the search as well.

March weather had been horrendous for viewing, and Olbers was chomping at the bit. Saturday the twenty-eighth, the skies finally cleared. The next evening he was happily ensconced in his attic lookout, immersed once again in the painstaking examination of Virgo, specifically the constellation's northerly "wing." As things turned out, he was not disappointed.

Two days later, he sent an excited letter to Schröter and his young assistant, Friedrich Bessel, revealing the discovery of what would become known as Vesta. Wilhelm Olbers had become the first and, for many years thereafter, the only man to discover two asteroids. His finding electrified the community of astronomers. Work on the sky search took on new urgency, only to be disastrously disrupted when, in 1813, Napoleon's retreat from Russia made its way through Lilienthal. The city was sacked and burned, the observatory looted. Schröter's notes and records were destroyed, and he died three years later, a broken man. Olbers kept searching until his death in 1840, but he never did find another asteroid.

On August 17, 2011, Dawn stopped by on its way to Ceres. The spacecraft spent seven months orbiting the little world, sending all manner of data back to its controllers on Earth. The mission was deemed a great success. At 326 miles in diameter, Vesta is the third-largest asteroid and by far the most interesting, with a fifteen-mile-deep crater, enormous peaks, and mineral components providing topography and composition unlike any other major asteroid. Rotating in just over 5.3 hours, its gravity is 7.4 times less than the Moon. Attractive for these and other reasons, Vesta called out to the boomers.

Forty years later, humans began arriving in large numbers, and by the twenty-second century it was home to over four million biological and electronic souls. Planetary culture was in many ways similar to that of Ceres. Vesta was a frontier world populated by boomers and their offspring, and the possibilities seemed endless.

~

On October 31, 2103, Darwin came calling. The same mystifying, horrific face that had been Meredith Sansone's last vision showed up in the skies of Olbers' second discovery. Many of those who actually saw the approach were convinced it was some zillionaire's prank; it was, after all, Halloween.

Surayya Fariq, a stringer for the *Luna Times,* happened to be visiting a friend on the job in Vesta Central's busy hub. She had seen reports from Mars on the peculiar circumstances of Phobos and quickly feared what might be coming. She composed a brief message to her home office, then had her friend send it via directed burst. Within minutes the scene overhead changed. The giant vessel released a glowing ball that expanded to envelope Vesta. The Halloween hypothesis began to look unlikely when VestaNet's primary nodes began to fail in rapid succession and when the remarkable planetoid's surface installations began to turn into dust. Surayya and her friend were among the first humans affected, watching each other in horrified fascination as they turned into dust.

The destruction of Vesta was accomplished within hours. Men, women, and children were reduced to ashes with no hope of rescue or resuscitation. All machine intelligence suffered the same fate. When it was over, a vibrant world on the cutting edge of civilization had turned into a 326-mile-wide ball of undifferentiated molecular junk.

26

Recently arrived on Zion, Quentin Adler happened to be in conversation with the chief of security when Darwin struck Vesta. He felt his awareness slip away, replaced by what felt like a waking dream with multiple points of view. The polyphonic voice he knew so well intoned in his head:

"Watch. Witness. Remember."

To Zion's security chief, seated across his desk and already dubious about Adler's strange tale, it appeared that his visitor was in the grip of a fugue or seizure of some kind. After making sure the big man was in no danger of injuring himself, the chief rang medical and asked for assistance. Zion was a small place, and its residents' macro- and nanoenhancements made it even smaller. Within minutes a medical team was on its way to their location, as were Morrie Siegel and his guest, their tour on hold. Adler was transported to the infirmary while the security chief briefed Siegel, who held a position of considerable respect within the asteroid's scientific community. Both Siegel and Cardinal Rauschman were intrigued. The story was incomplete but compelling, particularly given the reports from Mars.

To Adler, it seemed he was watching a multiplexed video. He saw Vesta from Darwin, he saw Darwin from Vesta, and he saw Vesta from within as its anguished final moments turned to silence. No escape, no defense, no relief. After several hours, he regained consciousness to find himself surrounded by medical and security personnel and others, including Siegel and Rauschman. Squinting against the bright overhead glowbars, he sat up with a haunted look on his face.

The security chief, an Israeli transplant of middle years named Lev Cohen, stepped forward and asked, "Mr. Adler, how are you feeling? You have been, ah, unconscious or something for over four hours." While he spoke, the attending medics measured vital signs and found no abnormalities. Meanwhile, Quentin looked around the room as if to reassure himself that he really was where he thought he was.

He said, "God help those people. God help all of us. I have some things to tell you, and it's going to take some time." Cohen, who had heard his description of the encounter with Darwin but knew nothing of Vesta, advised him to calm down and take his time before speaking. He introduced him to the attending physician, Siegel, and Rauschman then asked everyone else to leave the room. Quentin then told his story. The medical AI verified his truthfulness. Thirty minutes later, an ashen-faced Cohen led the others from the room.

Turning, he said, "You'll have to excuse me, Dr. Siegel, Eminence. I must go to Central. If Adler's story checks out, we must get word out immediately, then see about our own defenses." Cardinal Rauschman accompanied him, needing to get out messages of his own.

27

Morrie Siegel couldn't remember ever having been this excited. He wasn't ignoring or disputing the horrible events related back in the infirmary; rather, he was embracing one aspect of Adler's experience. Remote scan! It was almost too much to contemplate. Rushing along the main corridor, he entered the science labs at full steam and gathered up two assistants on the way to his office. Over the next forty minutes, he outlined a crash program to reverse-engineer and build such a technology. He didn't tell anyone his secret thought because he hardly dared admit it even to himself. He realized he missed Don Foster. At least with him he could depend on criticism without hidden agendas.

He thought back to the day he had first met Foster nearly seventy years earlier. They had found themselves sharing a table under a gigantic Oktoberfest tent in Munich. Foster had been surrounded by nieces and nephews. They were on a farewell holiday in their uncle's honor; his much-abused body was not responding to modern medicine, and his doctors had given him only a few months to live. Beer and schnapps had figured high on his list of remaining priorities.

Siegel had embraced the growing field of nanotechnology and had a theory about cellular replacement. In between steins of foaming brew, he explained what he had in mind. Foster didn't hesitate.

"Sign me up, Doc. I've got no more options, and I'm damned if I want to make it easy for these kids to inherit my measly savings."

Six months later, every cell in Foster's body had been replaced by a molecular analog. Barring a catastrophic accident, his nephews and nieces wouldn't have to deal with probate for quite some time to come. He still walked, talked, and looked like the old Don. He would soon learn, though, that he could alter his appearance at will and make his new body adapt to all manner of circumstances.

Siegel's assistants rushed off to work. They knew their obsessive master's moods well and understood that he expected instant results. Siegel, meanwhile, plunged into an extended computer modeling exercise using the lab's powerful AI to work out the theoretical basis for his impossible, secret thought. Forty-eight sleepless hours later, he had it.

28

The Planet Uncle Don was far behind and Vesta was still weeks away when John XXIV heard about the disaster ahead. Accompanied by Father Bertani and Cardinal Llewellyn, the captain had knocked on his door and delivered the news that Vesta, apparently, was no more.

"Your pardon, Holiness, but it has been confirmed by off-planet sources; the entire world was destroyed with all hands," the captain said in a disbelieving voice. The pope searched his face for evidence of—something?—then looked at Bertani and Llewellyn, both of whom nodded gravely.

"How can this be? An entire world, millions of souls?"

"Reports are sketchy, Holiness," Bertani said, "but it appears that the same vessel was involved in the attack on Phobos we recently heard about." The four men spent the next hour discussing events, trying to assimilate the information and what it might mean for them and for humanity. A visibly shaken Carolyn West joined them after hearing the news in the lounge and pointed out that, with their destination no longer available, the ferry needed to be redirected before it reached a point of no return. The captain agreed, noting that this part of the belt was rather sparsely settled, and that the only alternatives within range were TPUD, their previous stop, and Zion, Cardinal Rauschman's location.

"This is an easy choice," said the pope. "We go to Zion, fetch Josef, and continue on our way. Captain, please contact the local authority and request permission for such a stop. Thomas, please contact Josef and let him know of our change in plans. And Alberto, please set up the lounge for Mass. This is clearly a time for prayer." Carolyn offered to assist Bertani, and the group departed, leaving a thoughtful pontiff behind.

29

Long-distance communication had progressed little during the twenty-first century. The speed of electromagnetic waves continued to approximate three hundred thousand kilometers per second, and a Martian call for help or news flash could easily take fifteen or twenty minutes to reach Earth. Communiqués originating in the belt might not reach their destinations for hours. Children of the boomers in particular had trouble with this, since they had grown up on Earth accustomed to unlimited connectivity and virtually instant access to real-time information.

Nevertheless, Surayya Fariq's last report from Vesta did reach her home office and did, after minor editing delays, reach most of the Inner System. It followed by several weeks the inexplicable report of destruction on Phobos, and alarms began to sound as politicians, bloggers, and talking heads everywhere drew the inescapable conclusion that something terrible was descending on them. The lack of any data about the threat itself made it even more terrifying. A purported long-distance image of the attacker was also circulated, but it was widely debunked as a fraud due to its bizarre aspect.

Captain Charles Rooker tossed the newsfax at the flashcan in the corner, then rose and walked deliberately down Mars Central's main corridor to the supervisor's office. The events on Phobos weighed heavily on his mind, and now this! After Phobos, civilian authority on Mars had elected to hunker down and, in Rooker's mind, bury its collective head in the sand. There had been skepticism over his report, criticism over the losses, and no willingness to engage the enemy, whatever it was. *No more,* he thought. The Vesta report was persuasive beyond all possibility of denial.

He had a profound sense of unreality as Supervisor Antoinette Braley ushered him out of her office fifteen minutes later.

"Did you know," she observed with a hand on his arm, "Meredith and I were classmates at Penn State years ago? I still can't believe she's gone."

"I can imagine how you must feel, Supervisor, but can we go back to the Vesta report? Doesn't it seem clear to you that…" Rooker closed his mouth; he realized she had kept right on talking as though he had nothing to say.

"Captain, I trust that you will do what is necessary to keep us safe, nothing more. The Council's view is that our best strategy is the low-key approach. If we could make the entire planet invisible, we would do so." Rooker couldn't believe his ears. And he knew damn well that when she said "Council" she was blowing smoke at him and really meant herself.

He extricated himself from her grasp and headed back to security, never noticing the people who scurried out of his way upon seeing the big man's ramrod posture and thunderous visage. Donning VR gear, he engaged his enhancements, linking with MarsWeb, the Security AI, and all networked off-planet resources. He needed data. *More importantly,* he thought with some bitterness, *we need allies.* It seemed incredible, but the only way to avert disaster on his own world would be to find help elsewhere. His ability to deal with threats even with authorization was severely limited; no Inner System world other than Earth had any real military capability. But he had his three cruisers and a trained cadre. He had to do *some*thing, assuming he could track down the intruder. He began searching, though he was unclear about the search's objective. Two hours later, he found an anomaly; the tiny asteroid world of Ida had recently gone silent.

A communication hiatus originating in the belt was not normally a cause for concern, but Ida was a special case. The thirty-five-mile-long asteroid was discovered in 1884 by Austrian Johann Palisa; the deep-space Galileo probe visited and photographed the asteroid in 1993. It turned out Ida was binary. One hundred years later, its tiny satellite Dactyl was turned into the asteroid belt's first commercial radio station by an eccentric "shock jock" who had worn out his welcome back on Earth. The lengthy transmission times made the entire enterprise a bit anachronistic, and not surprisingly most of the belt ignored its 24/7 broadcasts. Until they stopped. Reports circulating on the Web and elsewhere were merely speculative, since no one had actually gone to take a look. As with most locations in the belt, Ida was remote and had few neighbors.

"Hell and damnation!" Swearing under his breath, Rooker sat back in frustration. He needed to get a line on the intruder's whereabouts, and it seemed that the only way to do so was to wait for the next attack. He needed to know where it was based, if it even had a base. That's when he remembered the buoys.

Back in the heady first days of expansion, Earth authorities had designed and deployed a ring of sensing devices around the Inner System, justifying the expense with talk of early warning, asteroid tracking, and scientific research. Carefully screened from public view was the fact that the whole system would be obsolete the day it was activated. Of course, it came out anyway amid reports of pork-barrel politics, and a powerful congressman ended up in a new line of work as a result of the "space buoy" scandals.

Rooker knew a great deal about the buoys; his uncle, the former congressman, had told him all about them while pumping gas and making change at the Peoria convenience mart. He snapped his fingers and beckoned a nearby orderly.

"Emerson, I need you to start searching buoy locations. Triangulate Vesta, Ida, and Phobos. Get me some reference points, pronto!" He returned to his own searching, only to be interrupted a minute later by the orderly's throat clearing.

"What is it?" Rooker barked.

The unfortunate Emerson stammered, "Sssir, buoys, sir? I, ah…ah…"

"Jesuschrist! Don't they teach you kids anything anymore?" Before Emerson could answer, Rooker composed himself.

"Put on your VR gear, and I'll hook you up with what you need to know. Now move it!"

With his assistant finally squared away, Rooker dove back into the electronic ether determined to track down the data he knew must be somewhere, probably on Earth. He checked the relative positions of the two planets to determine transmission lag and found he was in luck; Earth was near enough that the lag was only seven minutes. He got to work.

30

Daniel Kirkwood had been intrigued by the growing number of celestial bodies being discovered every year. Fortunately for astronomy, there was no observatory at Indiana University, which forced his excellent mind to absorb each new report and create a mental image in four dimensions. He was especially intrigued by the relative motions of planets and how they might affect each other. By 1866, there were over fifty known asteroids, and he knew as surely as the Sun rose each morning that Jupiter's gravity would have had massive, cumulative impacts on their paths. He was right.

There are almost no asteroids 2.5 astronomical units out from the Sun because that region's orbital resonance with Jupiter is exactly 1:3—its orbital period of 3.95 years is just one-third of Jupiter's. The gas giant's gravity has swept the area clean, propelling most local asteroids on long trips to parts unknown. Over millions of years, it has created the most dramatic of the Kirkwood Gaps, a lonely area in the midst of the belt's millions of fragments.

~

The construct known as Darwin moved through the Kirkwood Gap at an astonishing rate of speed. At perihelion, Ida had been conveniently close to the Gap and a useful proving ground for the next phase of the winnowing. Test successfully completed, the construct beamed electromagnetic modules at a random assortment of human settlements as it raced around the Sun. One such module found its way to TPUD-001.

31

Martha Ling had a decorator's eye, and her talent was evident everywhere. Jack had long admired the Hog and Hen's genuine pub ambiance, and the first time she invited him into her apartment he realized she cared tremendously about comfort and appearance. Furniture, fixtures, and finishes were all of the highest quality. He wondered briefly how anyone out in the belt could afford the transport costs that much of what he saw must have carried. He forgot about it fairly quickly, however. As he'd already discovered, his boss was short on patience when it came to affairs of the heart.

That morning they were propped up on pillows in a huge, luxurious bed. Jack thought the coffee might be the best he'd ever had.

Martha wasn't quite purring as she said, "Have some of this, Jack. You need to keep up your strength." Covered only partially by the sheet, Martha was feeding him morsels of sumptuous banana nut bread with cream cheese when with a wet crack! the top of her head exploded. Bits of brain, blood, and bone spattered his face and chest. Moments later, Jack realized that the shattering wail in his ears was his own screaming, and he began to shake violently as he struggled for control. What remained of Martha was slumped over, already barely resembling human form.

As he scrambled out of bed and into his clothes, he became aware that something was wrong with the room. The ceiling appeared to be drooping in the middle, and as he watched, the droop elongated into a column that detached itself from ceiling and floor and morphed into a humanoid figure. Feeling some relief at this point because it was clear he was only having a nightmare, Jack was dismayed when the figure turned and took a step toward him. It had no eyes, no ears, no mouth. But there was no mistaking the animus as it came after him.

Jack was even more convinced of the nightmare scenario when the floor turned into a giant hand that grasped the humanoid and squeezed it until the head and limbs dropped off and the torso imploded. Just before he blacked out, conviction became certainty when the fingers of the hand merged and turned into Uncle Don Foster.

~

"Jack? Jack? Jack! Wake your sorry ass up and talk to me!"

Reality returned with a rush, and Jack opened his eyes to find a very worried-looking Don Foster bending over him with a glass in hand.

"Drink this," he ordered, and Jack automatically swallowed the clear fluid without thinking. He finally stopped choking and gasping for air two minutes later, tears streaming down his face, and was able to describe the recent events to Foster and Angela Ford, who was standing nearby.

Finishing, he said, "I know this sounds crazy, but it looked like the floor just squeezed this thing to pieces, and then you were there. I dunno, I dunno...Martha..." He squeezed his eyes shut, but when he opened them the scene was unchanged. Don and Angela looked at each other, then Foster spoke.

"Angie, as far as I can tell, that was the only one. Get a couple of the boys to take care of Martha and deal with the room. We'll be at the pub when you're done."

A few minutes later, sitting on a barstool, Jack learned all about Don's ability to manipulate his molecular structure and effectively move through walls or even solid rock. The Planet Uncle Don was literal truth. The man was the planet, and vice versa.

With some hesitation he said, "So, the hand coming out of the floor, that really was you?"

"Yessir," Don replied, "been wanting to try that trick out for a long time. But I sure didn't want to lose Martha along the way." Jack still couldn't quite wrap his mind around what had happened.

"So then what was that thing, and what happened to Martha?"

"That thing was some kind of terror machine programmed to shock and panic people by killing with maximum collateral impact. It would've chased you out into the corridor, then gone after others until the whole place was in an uproar. Like me, it could disassociate and go anywhere."

"But why blow someone's head up?" Don grimaced, then poured himself another brain softener.

"That's the only way to kill anyone these days. Everyone on this world has Enduring Life, or something like it. In the old days, you might shoot, stab, poison, or strangle whoever you were trying to kill, but none of those work anymore. You have to destroy the brain cells and neurobots."

After a pause, Jack said, "OK, I get that. So the sixty-four-dollar question becomes, where did that thing come from?"

"Yeah, that's the question all right. I know it came from somewhere in the Gap. I felt it hit a couple of hours ago, but it took me until it attacked you to actually find it and figure out what it was." Foster was thoughtful for a moment, then said, "I need Morrie. Excuse me, Jack."

Standing, he strode toward the exit, then turned back with a wry smile and said, "Guess the cat's out of the bag anyway." As Jack watched, he melted into the floor and disappeared, leaving him to ponder the fact that Martha was completely, irretrievably gone, just when he'd begun to get to know her. Acceptance would take time.

32

The planet shuddered. Virtually an organism itself, Ceres felt the "impacts" as several of Darwin's electromagnetic pulses reached the world and used local materials to transform themselves. Felt the impacts but was unable to characterize them. A vague unease spread through the Net as both the primary nodes and security worked overtime; a solution was problematic without more data. They didn't have long to wait.

Roger Tenbright was rather pleased with himself. An unrepentant boomer, he'd worked long and hard to re-create the sixties, and now owned and managed a nightclub that boasted a waiting line every night. The Cosmic Fillmore was the place to be.

On this night, Tenbright was especially pleased to have a noteworthy live act on stage for the first time. He'd managed to entice the surviving members of the Grateful Dead to make the trip and had booked them for a four-week gig. Runaway ticket sales had confirmed the wisdom of the move. He hummed along as the band performed "Truckin'."

Dallas—got a soft machine
Houston—too close to New Orleans
New York—got the ways and means
but just won't let you be.

He was admiring a statuesque redhead out on the dance floor, the same woman he'd been flirting with earlier as the club opened. He'd begun to consider the prospect of a mutual workout on the sofa in his office when her head exploded. Shocked speechless, he continued to watch as the people in her immediate vicinity reacted with horror, then screams as his burly security team pushed through the crowd toward the disturbance. The band continued playing until one of its members likewise lost his head. When two security officers' heads exploded like overripe fruit, the stampede was on.

As Tenbright stood watching the melee in disbelief, he observed a figure in the middle of the club, motionless except for an arm that pointed at various exploding heads. This seemed like important information, though he wasn't sure what to do with it. His neurocytes uplinked with CeresWeb just moments before the arm swung his way with predictable results.

The scene was repeated in clubs all over Ceres. The Net identified the locations and dispatched assistance, but it took most of the night to neutralize what the media quickly dubbed the "Torchers." When it was all over, nearly three thousand Ceresians had actually *died*—a trauma from which the planet might never recover.

33

Dachau, Third Reich, 1943—Cold and exhaustion began to give way to apprehension as the train slowed. Barely able to stand, Carl watched through the bars of the cattle car as the arrival platform slid into view. Above, a large, weathered sign read "Dachau." *Out of the frying pan and into the fire,* he thought bitterly. To have survived Auschwitz only to come to this was just too much to bear. At his feet, a young woman vomited while others attempted to shuffle away, though the crowd prevented any real movement. Eight bodies were stacked at one end, the unfortunates who hadn't survived the trip. He wondered, though, if perhaps they'd had the best of it.

He watched as the cars were moved onto a siding and pulled through town. He saw the snowcapped watchtowers first, then the fences and moat. *No question,* he thought as black-clad SS troopers opened the doors, *I have come to hell.*

They exited under the watchful eyes of the guards. Carl noticed a well-dressed man, small in stature but with obvious authority, who seemed to be directing the guards to separate the prisoners into two lines. Naturally curious, he made a mistake. He looked directly at the man, who was preoccupied with a young girl at the moment. Other than a faint hint of distaste, the face showed no emotion. Before he could see anymore, Carl collapsed to his knees as a nearby trooper struck his lower back with the butt of his rifle. Groaning, he struggled back to his feet.

"Dr. Rascher?" said the guard.

The strange little man glanced at Carl without emotion, the eyes as small, cold, and hard as a venomous snake's. "Baracke X," he replied. X Barracks.

Carl followed the young girl in line as they trudged across a bridge over a swiftly flowing stream. The man behind him said it was the Würm River. A low, brick building came into view ahead, and the prisoners were directed to enter a delousing room and remove all clothing. Typhus was rampant in all the camps, and Carl was unsurprised by the order. He felt momentary regret for the embarrassed girl; she obviously was new to the camps and had no experience with their dehumanizing effect. He thought briefly of his own daughter, safe, he hoped, in England. They were directed through a door into a gang shower where the delousing would be completed before they were issued camp clothes. The door closed with a solid clang. In respect for each other's privacy the prisoners looked everywhere but at each other as they waited for the overhead spray to begin.

As he waited, Carl's headache worsened, and he began to feel acute pain in his eyes. Rubbing them, he was startled by a moan from the girl, followed by her sudden collapse. He turned to her in concern but before he could act, another and then another of the prisoners collapsed. His chest tightened, and he found he couldn't seem to get any air into his lungs. His head began to spin as he felt drawn inexorably down into a vortex, and his last sensation before losing consciousness was the smell of bitter almonds.

Morrie slowly removed his VR gear and sat back at his console. He had thought he would feel jubilation or at least satisfaction when this moment arrived, but this felt more like weary anticlimax. The voice of his young assistant broke into his thoughts.

"Dr. Siegel? Do you think…?"

"Yes, yes, Benjamin, I think we got him. I'm not quite sure what we're going to do with him, may God forgive me, but I do think we got him. Carl Herschberg, born in Bonn in 1919, died at Dachau in 1943. Except now he lives as an upload right here on Zion. My grandfather."

Behind him, Cardinal Josef Rauschman stirred in his chair. Invited by Siegel to witness the test, the cardinal's face was a study in conflict. Thinking that he was about to observe historical events had been disturbing enough, but the enormity of what Siegel had actually accomplished left him speechless. The Church had never accepted uploads, treating the entire phenomenon as a misguided application of high technology in direct contravention of traditional Christian principles. It raised profoundly troubling questions about the nature of life, death, and the immortal soul. But these, Rauschman knew, didn't even begin to get at the heart of the matter before him now.

Siegel turned to Rauschman and said, "Josef, come have dinner with me. It will be some hours before we can attempt to communicate with my grandfather, and you must be at least as troubled as I am."

"Well, I suppose we must eat," conceded the cardinal as he rose. After briefly instructing his assistants, Siegel joined him, and the two men left for a nearby cafe. As they proceeded up the same corridor Siegel had come rushing down three days earlier, they were accosted by a security officer who handed them each hard copy of incoming message traffic.

The young woman, whose name tag read K. Oppenheimer, said, "Your pardon, Dr. Siegel, Eminence, but we had been given word you were not to be disturbed via link, so Colonel Cohen sent me over to deliver these." She stood by as the men read their messages. Rauschman finished first, waiting for Siegel and then telling him the papal ferry had changed course and would be arriving to pick him up in three days.

Siegel excused himself and said, "I must contact Don Foster at once. There's been an incident on TPUD, and these things may all be connected somehow. I'll meet you in the café in thirty minutes." With that, he rushed off with the security officer, and Rauschman continued on his way to the restaurant.

Arriving, he was chagrined to find that all of the tables were occupied by diners. He was about to leave when he saw Quentin Adler sitting at a corner table alone, waving him over.

"Eminence, please feel free to join me if you'd like. This place seems to be busy every time I pass this way."

Rauschman hesitated only briefly before he sat down, saying, "Much appreciated, Mr. Adler. I haven't seen you since the day in the infirmary. How have you been feeling?"

"Like I need to get out of here," he said. "What I *should* do is finish my run to Deimos and look for a return load. What I'd *like* to do is head back to Pallas. What I'll end up doing is anybody's guess." He shook his head in obvious frustration.

"Having heard your story, I quite understand your ambivalence," the cardinal said with some feeling. "Still, events seem to be converging here for some reason. You might want to bide your time on Zion until we know more about this Darwin." He told Adler that Morrie Siegel would be joining them shortly and suggested he stay to hear the latest news. Adler agreed.

After placing his order, Rauschman was about to say more when he felt something soft brush against his leg. When he looked down, he found a cat at his feet.

"Don't mind him," Adler said, "that's my ship's cat, Flick. He's going a bit stir-crazy too."

34

Much to the chagrin of her regulars, Sarah closed the Rockpile every Monday. She knew she needed at least one day a week to herself, and since they were the smallest groups, Monday crowds were the easiest to do without. This particular Monday she had planned a relaxed evening in order to have dinner with Rance Lee, whom she planned to marry in a few weeks. A miner, Rance had been courting Sarah for over two years. Even though his work occasionally took him well into the belt, he was seldom gone more than a month. He called Pallas home.

Rance appeared at her door on time and offered a bright smile as he leaned in for a kiss. A frown momentarily creased his face as Sarah offered cheek rather than lips, but he recovered quickly.

"Hello, darling, may I take you away to a five-course French dinner with the finest Bordeaux you'll ever have on Pallas?" Even though she ran a tavern, or perhaps because of it, Sarah had become an aficionado of high-end red wines. With the sole exception of Guinness, she found herself unable to drink most of the malted and distilled beverages her customers consumed in prodigious quantities. The invitation would normally have thrilled her, but tonight it left her cold.

"Rance, come in and sit for a minute." He followed her into the small but comfortable living area, then flopped on the sofa while she ducked into the kitchen for two glasses and an open bottle of Syrah.

After pouring and some idle conversation, she said, "I've done a lot of thinking lately. I know this is not fair to you, but I'm just not ready to get married."

Rance's face clouded.

"If this is about Adler," he said, "then you may never be ready to get married, to me or anyone else. I've heard enough to know something happened between you two. It's none of my business, but I've heard he's in some kind of trouble now."

"A lot less happened than you probably think, but you're right about one thing; it is about him, and until I settle things with him one way or another, I'd just be fooling both of us if I went ahead with the wedding."

A proud man, the miner stood with a carefully neutral expression on his face and said, "Let me know. I'll be waiting, for a little while anyway." Wine forgotten, he let himself out.

Sarah sat and finished her wine. Then, muttering "freaking men," she finished his.

~

In a small stateroom on a distant ferry, Carolyn West tossed and turned in the dark of the sleep cycle. The peaceful serenity that seemed to surround the pontiff eased most of her days even as crises loomed, but at night the demons she'd thought long buried once again disturbed her rest. And to top it off she had begun to wonder if she might have a vocation. The thought of her leading a religious life brought alternating bouts of despair and curiosity, but she knew that a future without meaning would kill her as surely as the vacuum of space.

35

It took awhile, but Rooker found the buoys. It was actually the hapless Emerson who finally tracked them down using a self-replicating search worm that blanketed the entire Inner System within hours. It seemed the kid had his uses after all, thought Rooker. The buoys were still deployed, and nearly 80 percent of them were still producing signal even after decades of non-maintenance.

The signals were archived in a database on Luna, not Earth, as Rooker had expected. Earthbound military authorities still controlled access to the data, although few of them seemed to be aware of its existence, or care, once Rooker reminded them. He was finally able to locate a colonel who understood the urgency of his request and took it up the chain of command. Access was granted by some nameless denizen of the Pentagon with the proviso that he share any useful intelligence. Acting quickly, he sifted the archive for buoy records in the vicinity of the attacks, then went looking for tracking data of any kind.

"Emerson, I need you to get busy with the AI and reduce this gibberish to pictures I can show the people who need to be convinced. I want history, and I want a forward projection with timelines."

"Sir! Right away, sir," the orderly replied crisply. He didn't want to face the consequences of disappointing his rather demanding superior.

When Emerson brought him the charts two hours later, Rooker sat back in disbelief. The pattern of destruction was clear enough, but the elapsed times indicated speeds that should have been untenable in the Inner System. And then there was the forward projection.

"This thing's got to be using the Gaps to get around," he said, "but it's still moving way too fast. There's no way to catch up with it. All anyone can do is anticipate its next move and put together a reception committee."

The forward projection showed perhaps a dozen settlements in and around the belt that were at high short-term risk, given the intruder's pattern thus far. Further in the future, all major and minor worlds were shown at risk. Rooker called his small staff together.

"People, take a real good look at these charts. You saw what this thing did to Phobos, and you've heard what it's doing elsewhere. We need to get on the air right now and contact every security authority we can find, starting with these twelve. Split 'em up and get busy. Send the charts and the backup data, and make these people believe you. I'll take Earth."

"Sir," one aide said, raising a hand, "what are we advising them to *do*?"

"I don't have a good answer for that," Rooker replied. "They should keep watch and take whatever defensive measures they can. Divert power to shielding. Deploy mines. Whatever. And pray. Any of these twelve could get hit during the next twenty-four hours."

Standing to leave, the four men and women quickly divided the settlements among themselves. Emerson sat at his desk to make his first contact, the tiny world of Zion.

36

Morrie Siegel was a troubled man. He had just left security after hearing all about the incident on TPUD from Don Foster. Reports from Ceres confirmed that on almost any other world the intruders would have run amok with devastating results. He was unable to see any other connection, though, between Foster's experience and the strange disturbances being reported elsewhere. And Quentin Adler's story still required explanation as well.

Mostly, however, he was disturbed because his moment of greatest triumph also seemed to be a moment of great crisis. He resented the distraction when all he wanted to do was focus on the promise of his temporal displacement project. Entering the café, he spotted Rauschman and Adler at a corner table and joined them.

Adler said, "Hello, Dr. Siegel. I hope your work is going well."

Glancing at Rauschman, who subtly shook his head, Siegel said, "Well enough, though there seem to be bigger things happening these days." He went on to tell the two men about the incident on TPUD and the news from Ceres, leaving out no details.

Rauschman crossed himself saying, "I mourn the loss of Ms. Ling. She was a marvelous hostess, very accommodating, very solicitous."

"I don't know anything about these latest things," said Adler. "If they're connected to Darwin, they're something new, I'm afraid."

Flick chose that moment to jump up onto Siegel's lap. Startled, Siegel quickly recovered and proved himself a cat lover by stroking the feline and eliciting a prolonged purr. Flick settled down as if to stay, and the men resumed their conversation.

"Hmmm, what might this be?" Siegel was fingering a small rectangular object attached to Flick's collar.

Adler looked closely, then said, "I have no idea. He always wears his collar, but I've never seen that before. It almost looks like a miniature data card."

"I believe you're right, Quentin. I'm thinking we should head back to the lab and find out what, if anything, is on it."

"And where it came from," added Rauschman.

Both questions were answered a short while later. Siegel was able to find a port that would accept the card in his lab, and the others watched as he powered up a link to the AI that coordinated most of the lab's work. The AI reported that the card had an internal power supply and that there was in fact something on the card. It then reported that the code was archaic and might take some effort to unravel. A few minutes later, the men were startled to hear a voice over the system's speakers.

"About time somebody figured this out! I finally get myself out of that godforsaken place, and you let me hang around a cat, for cryin' out loud!" That the speaker was irritated was evident, but identity remained a mystery. Siegel recovered first.

"Excuse me for being obtuse, but we have no idea who you are or where you came from. Would you care to enlighten us? I'm Morrie Siegel, by the way, and my two associates are Quentin Adler and Cardinal Josef Rauschman."

"Pleased to meet you all," said the voice. "I am, or at least was, Harry Grosvenor, formerly a dentist from Ann Arbor, Michigan, and until recently an unwilling resident on Sanctuary. Or what Mr. Adler here knows as Darwin."

37

The ceremony was brief but well attended. Martha had touched the lives of almost everyone on TPUD, and the finality of her passing cast a somber pall over the gathering in the Hog and Hen. Still in a bit of a daze, Jack served as an unobtrusive usher, making sure people had seats and refreshments.

A woman Jack didn't know walked to the front of the assembly and led the memorial. She was effective in combining traditional recitals with observations about Martha. Near the end, she invited anyone who wished to speak to come forward, and a procession of friends, employees, and customers told stories or said public farewells. Jack stood mute, unable to muster the will. Finally, Don Foster took the podium.

"Martha was one of our best and brightest. She came out here early, when there was no particular reason to think we'd succeed. She stayed out here, even after our marriage ended, because she still cared about everyone in this room and believed in what we were doing. And now she'll stay out here forever in our hearts."

"Amen," chorused most of those in the room.

As Foster resumed his seat and the service wound to a close, Jack was shaking his head. Did I hear right? Were they married? He had to set aside further thought in order to exchange farewells as mourners began to file past on their way out the door. Finally, most were gone.

"Jack, snap out of it. We've got work to do."

He looked around and discovered a handful of people still in the bar clustered around Foster. Joining them, he was surprised to hear Angela Ford report that the papal ferry had turned back and was on its way to Zion to pick up Cardinal Rauschman.

"They'll actually pass quite close on their way by," she continued. "The diversion time would add up to four hours at most."

"Hmph," said Foster. "After my little chat with Morrie, it's pretty clear that Zion is where the action is right now."

Angela said, "There's something else. Mars Central has been in touch. Somehow, they've tracked the vessel that's causing all the destruction and forecast its next moves. We're on the list of secondary targets, which puts us at serious risk. Zion is on the list of primaries. They could get hit any time."

Foster began swearing under his breath as he lit up a cigarette, then said, "We need somebody over there to protect our interests, help out if they can. Why don't you ask the Holy Father's captain to swing by here for a pickup?"

As the security officer left, Foster turned and said, "Can you do anything useful, Jack? Besides making brain softeners, I mean. It seems we're all going to be stretched in new directions for a while, and we need help."

"I'm basically a navigator, boss. Got my training at RPI and worked the Moon runs for a few years before I got out to run my charter business."

Looking at him speculatively, Foster said, "How do you feel about going over to Zion for a few days? With the threat level so high, I'm thinking I need to stay here and work on some kind of defense with Angela. I'd feel a lot better if someone with a good head on his shoulders was closer to the center of things."

"Of course," Jack said, though he wasn't sure why he was rushing into danger. Changing the subject, he said, "What will happen now with the Hog and Hen?"

"It'll be closed for a while out of respect to Martha, then we'll have to find someone to reopen the place." Foster looked glum as he contemplated the near future without his favorite tavern. "Put some gear together, Jack. Angela's messaging me that your ride will be docking in three hours. And I've got some notes to write."

"Okeydoke," Jack said, "I'm out of here."

38

Earth, especially the North Americans and Chinese, had always dominated the Special Treaty Organization for Interplanetary Cooperation, known to most as STOIC. Seemingly irrelevant much of the time, STOIC had taken very seriously the attacks that led to Rooker's warning. Ships had been redeployed from bases on the Moon and from Earth's orbit shortly after Phobos was destroyed. Even now a mini-armada was approaching the Gap.

Back on Mars, Rooker was not pleased. His civilian overseers had required him to stand down, though they did allow one of his cruisers to join the STOIC fleet. He was also unhappy with STOIC's tactical approach. Its commanders dismissed the data that indicated high speeds as "improbable" and "unreliable" even as they used Rooker's forecasting to plot an intercept vector. They expected to engage and destroy the intruder far from any settled worlds.

On the bridge of the STOIC flagship, the *Shanghai*, Lieutenant Song Chen turned in his seat to report to the fleet commander.

"Admiral Jiang, all ships report that they are on-station. The formation is complete as ordered."

For the first time in weeks, the dour, impassive face of China's most senior space commander actually smiled.

Jiang had dutifully accepted the mission; she was, after all, a third-generation military officer who knew better than to question orders. She had known from the start, though, that the journey would be tedious and have little chance of success. Find a vessel in the asteroid belt? She was unconvinced by the Martians' logic, yet here they were, taking up station millions of kilometers from anywhere worthwhile. At least the Americans and Europeans had more or less behaved themselves; the last thing she needed was a career-wrecking international incident. Now they would wait.

"Instruct all ships to optimize in scan-and-response mode. I want cross-linkage in place immediately. Let's get the Net working and see what comes our way."

"Aye, sir."

In short order, coordinated activities were under way on all six ships of the fleet as they waited for their quarry.

Researchers in the U.S. and Britain have unveiled their blueprints for building a cloaking device.

So far, cloaking has been confined to science fiction; in Star Trek it is used to render spacecraft invisible. Professor Sir John Pendry says a simple demonstration model that could work for radar might be possible within eighteen months' time. In the journal Science two separate teams, including Professor Pendry's, have outlined ways to cloak objects.

These research papers present the maths required to verify that the concept could work. But developing an invisibility cloak is likely to pose significant challenges.

Both groups propose methods using the unusual properties of so-called "metamaterials" to build a cloak. These metamaterials can be designed to induce a desired change in the direction of electromagnetic waves, such as light. This is done by tinkering with the nano-scale structure of the metamaterial, not by altering its chemistry.
BBC News, May 25, 2006

Time passed. Jiang had been ordered to take up position, intercept, and destroy the intruder. The limiting factors of food, water, and air would eventually force their hand, but she knew she was likely to be stuck in place for several weeks. The six ships were arranged on the circumference of a theoretical sphere, the center point of which sat directly on Rooker's highest-probability vector. Sensors directed by on-board AIs maintained a vigilant watch, even when human crews required rest.

It was the nadir of a sleep cycle, silent, dark, and motionless on board the U.S. cruiser *Houston*. Except for the two-man watch, most of the crew slept. The *Houston* was a relatively small ship whose chief attributes were speed and maneuverability. A single corridor joined the bridge with crew quarters, mess, support, and engineering; there was no wasted space. Its crew was comfortable, but cramped.

Lieutenant John Brooks, ship commander, was on the bridge reading a briefing report about the recent improbable events on Ceres and TPUD when he heard a noise behind him. He turned in the command chair just in time to see his radioman's head explode, splattering gore in all directions. Appalled, he slapped an alarm button as his training took over, next reaching for a sidearm. Claxons began sounding throughout the ship as the AI's voice instructed crew to arm themselves and take up battle stations immediately.

Seeing no one else on the bridge, Brooks instructed the AI by name, "Seven, contact the *Shanghai* and fill them in. I've got to brief the crew."

He headed down the main corridor expecting to encounter his men, only to find an eerie absence of activity. Bursting through the door into quarters, he nearly slipped and went down on the slick deck, bright red blood and gore everywhere he looked. Whatever had killed his radioman had already been here. All dead.

Brooks headed back toward the bridge. A half dozen steps from the entry, he stopped cold. A face in the surface of the door looked back at him without expression. He shivered briefly as he realized it was the coldest, most inhuman look he'd ever seen. As if stepping through the door, the face became an entire figure as it came toward him and raised an arm to point at his head. It had to be one of these so-called Torchers. He knew what was coming and shouted: "Seven, autodestruct gamma execute!"

Six hundred miles away, Lieutenant Song had just rung the admiral's cabin to update her on the strange occurrences aboard the *Houston* when the main screen lit up with a blinding flash. Sensors confirmed that the *Houston* had exploded. As Song sounded general quarters and the admiral reached the bridge, sensors reported something else as well: a huge, metallic orb had just appeared in the middle of the containment bubble as if from nowhere.

"Ta ma de!" Oh shit! Nonplussed, Song reverted to street slang as the screen focused on the intruder. Autoroutines on the five remaining ships immediately launched bombs, missiles, and energy pulses at the sphere, all of which raced off aimlessly into deep space as the sphere disappeared. Then, ship by ship, the doomed fleet began to disintegrate as the huge globe reappeared briefly next to each, engulfed it with iridescent clouds of nanoreducers, and disappeared once again.

Last to be accosted was the Martian cruiser *Lowell*. All activity on the bridge came to a halt as the giant vessel shimmered into view no more than five thousand yards away. Transfixed by the sight of a ten-kilometer death's-head glaring out of her main screen, Lieutenant Ayala Denton felt the blood drain from her face. A few feet away at the fire-control console, crewman Elston Rodriguez watched in frustration as the last of his missiles tracked toward the globe, then disappeared.

Astonishingly, the face on the screen began to twist out of shape and then seemed nearly to be displaced by a second face. Denton watched in disbelief as the mammoth visage began rapid morphing.

"Diablo!" Hernandez exclaimed. "It is as if the creature is at war with itself!"

"Let's get out of here," said Denton to her pilot. The young ensign needed no further encouragement, engaging the main drives in record time.

"Plot us the shortest course out of the Gap, then get me a list of the closest settlements." She thought further, then added, "And get me a line to Mars Central. I need to talk to the captain ASAP." Rooker needed to be brought into this, she thought. As soon as possible.

Many miles astern, the construct known as Darwin remained immobile. To outward appearances, faces continued to rage across its surface as if doing battle with each other. Hours passed, and the changes began to slow. Finally they stopped, settling once more into the skeletal death's-head. As if awakening, the giant vessel resumed its journey, passing through the center of the former containment bubble, now just an expanding cloud of space junk.

39

Work in the lab had come to a standstill as everyone got acquainted with Harry Grosvenor. Not quite garrulous, he nonetheless had an intricate story to tell about his early years on Sanctuary and the subsequent decades with Darwin.

At one point Adler interrupted, "Are you saying there are others like you, Doctor? Other uploads who don't buy into this so-called winnowing that's going on?"

"Of course I'm saying that, you idiot! There are something like eleven million uploads on Darwin. We're not all crazy. Just, unfortunately, most of us."

"Which means," said Siegel, "there's no way to take back control."

"That is an unfortunate fact," said Grosvenor. "It explains why I decided to take advantage of Mr. Adler and his feline friend. It was the only way I could think of to get the hell out of Dodge and have a chance of preserving my, ah, electronic skin, as it were."

Before Adler could ask what "Dodge" meant, Zion's security chief Lev Cohen broke in.

"Dr. Grosvenor, can you confirm or expand on what Mr. Adler has told us about Darwin's intentions?"

"Oh, the intention is clear enough. Darwin intends to destroy all biological human life in the solar system.

If a few million uploads get wiped out along the way, that'll be acceptable collateral damage. Darwin has come to believe that it not only represents the next stage of human evolution, but that it's responsible for ensuring that the species takes the necessary step to get there." The room became very quiet as the full weight of this message sank in.

Cardinal Rauschman had said little during the exchange, preferring to listen and think about what he was hearing. He'd had very few conversations with uploads over the years. Many in the Church considered them an abomination, contrary to God's laws and traditional Church teachings. He knew they would point to Darwin as proof of their point of view.

Rauschman's ambivalence was rooted in his own early experience with macro- and nanoenhancements, experience that had taught him something of their intrinsic ability to elevate the human condition. Despite his apparent orthodoxy, he had never been comfortable dismissing such advances out of hand. It was one reason he supported the pontiff even as he sometimes gave the opposite public impression. A bit of Curial misdirection was occasionally required, if only to keep the real opponents of progress off base. *Besides,* he thought with amusement, *it was fun.*

The group was breaking up. Cohen made arrangements to debrief Grosvenor more thoroughly after conversing with his superiors, and Adler left on his own errands after bidding everyone good-bye. Morrie Siegel turned to Rauschman.

"Josef, I think the time has come to attempt communication with my grandfather. Are you game to listen in?"

"Of course, Morrie. We have come this far. I must see this through. I was wondering, though, if Dr. Grosvenor might be of some help in this matter."

Siegel brightened. "What a marvelous idea! I had prepared a simple VR environment for him, but contact with another electronic intelligence may indeed ease the transition."

∾

Aware that time must have passed, he was startled to realize he had any awareness at all. He had no doubt what the smell of bitter almonds had meant, but now he seemed to be in a room, a parlor with comfortable overstuffed furniture and a fire burning in a large hearth. *So, this is the answer to the greatest mystery of all?* he wondered. *Yes, there is life after death, and it looks like my uncle's living room?*

A door swung open, and an older, well-dressed man walked in. He looked around with some bemusement, then said "Nice job, Morrie," before noticing Carl for the first time.

"Mr. Herschberg, I presume?" Not trusting himself to speak, Carl nodded.

"Mr. Herschberg, my name is Harry Grosvenor. I'm a dentist from Michigan, in the United States. I understand you're originally from Bonn, more recently from Auschwitz and Dachau. Do I have that right?"

Carl nodded again, his head now full of questions. God was a dentist?

"Please sit down, Mr. Herschberg. We have some catching up to do."

Siegel was pacing. To Rauschman's astonishment, he shakily fumbled a pack of cigarettes out of a pocket and lit up, inhaling deeply. After a moment he breathed out a cloud of blue smoke.

Somewhat sheepishly he said, "I can't remember ever feeling anything like this. I know you're conflicted, Josef, but you have to admit, this is big."

"Perhaps bigger than anything," Rauschman replied. "I hope you're thinking about consequences, my friend."

Before Siegel could reply, a voice from the speakers said, "Gentlemen? I believe we've accomplished the preliminaries here, and I'd like to introduce you to someone. Cardinal Rauschman, may I present a countryman of yours, Carl Herschberg? And Carl, that rather anxious-looking fellow sitting next to the cardinal there is your grandson, Morrie Siegel."

After a slight pause, another voice said, "Very pleased to meet you, Cardinal. And especially pleased to meet you, Grandson. Grandson? Morrie?"

The cardinal interrupted, "I'm sorry, Carl, give us just a moment, will you? It seems your grandson has fainted."

40

Adler had left the lab because he'd seen something in the Rooker report he wanted to check out. He returned to Zion Central and searched for Lev Cohen without success. Recognizing him, a young security officer at a nearby desk introduced herself and asked whether he needed assistance.

"Yes, I do, Officer. I've been through Captain Rooker's report and wanted to run some plots, in particular looking at Pallas. It's far enough off the ecliptic that they may have missed it the first time around, but this thing's speed makes everybody a target." He would have returned to his ship for this exercise, but he wanted access to the detail and power in the Zion system.

The officer showed Adler to a VR console not in use, then set him up with access to the navigation routines and ephemerides he would need for his analysis.

"Let me know if I can be of any further assistance."

"Thanks," Adler said. "Would you let me know if Lev comes in?"

"Of course, I'll send him right over."

Adler settled in for what he knew might be a lengthy skull session. Donning a VR headset, he called up Rooker's report just to review its forecasts one more time. Highest-risk settlements were highlighted in bright red. He had a sudden thought and sent an inquiry to the labs. A few minutes later he was joined in virtual reality by Harry Grosvenor.

"Dr. Grosvenor? I wonder if you'd take a look at this data and tell me whether it syncs with your own knowledge of Darwin's intentions?"

Grosvenor replied, "Be glad to, but remember Darwin isn't completely rational. Whatever we might deduce, it might just as easily do something completely off the charts.

"Hmmm. This is pretty good. By the way, I think you can all take Zion off the list of primaries, if only because you're here now and Darwin won't want to eliminate its official witness." Only slightly reassured, Adler called up the ephemerides. Pallas was still somewhat above the ecliptic and away from the Gaps, so it did not appear on Rooker's list of targets.

"Can you tell me anything about Pallas, Doctor? Was there any reason it might either be skipped or specifically targeted?"

Taking a closer look, Grosvenor said, "I see why you're concerned. Pallas is a huge settlement, and not well defended. Not that Darwin cares about defenses. All I can tell you is that Darwin will most likely divert out of the main belt to eliminate Pallas, but I can't tell you when or where. We could predict that it would happen the first time one of Rooker's vectors juxtaposes with its current orbit. When will that be?"

After running the required calculations Adler said, "Three weeks and three days from now, all other things being equal. Thanks, Doc, but I gotta go." He ripped off the VR headset, and as he stood to leave, Lev Cohen appeared in the doorway, a grim look on his face.

"Mr. Adler, I'm sorry to tell you this, but we are impounding your ship. You cannot be allowed to leave Zion so long as your presence here ensures our continued survival."

Stunned, Adler sat back down. "You can't be serious. I have to get back to Pallas."

"That's not going to happen right now, my friend. You have my sympathies, but I hope you understand my position; I have to do everything possible to protect this world."

Adler was a big man. It crossed his mind that he could probably overpower Cohen, leave Central, and quickly make his way to his ship. He rose to make his move, but before he could do anymore he felt himself overwhelmed once again by what he was starting to call the "witness effect." This time the multiple points of view showed him the destruction of the fleet, ending with the *Lowell's* escape.

When Adler collapsed, Cohen recognized the symptoms and called medical. They made Adler as comfortable as possible while they waited anxiously to hear about whatever he was being shown. When Adler did come out of his trance a few hours later, the authorities on Zion were the first to learn of the fleet's destruction. After relating his newest story, Adler learned that he was now a "guest" of Zion and would be accompanied by an official escort everywhere he went. He was not a happy man.

41

The ride from TPUD to Zion had been uneventful for Jack except for two chance meetings. The first had been with the Holy Father himself as Jack had transited a corridor looking for the exercise room. Once the hulking Swiss guard had satisfied himself that Jack posed no threat, he was allowed to stand respectfully as the pontiff passed by going the other way.

John XXIV greeted him warmly, saying, "Captain, it is a pleasure to see you again, though I much regret the circumstances that brought us together. We remember Miss Ling in our prayers."

"Thank you, Holiness."

Jack watched him disappear down the hall, not really seeing him as Martha's death replayed in his mind's eye. After a moment, he continued on to the gym.

Which is where he literally bumped into Carolyn West as he entered and she exited the "tank," an Earth-normal gravity room with exercise equipment designed to tone and strengthen muscles. To save expense, long-distance ferries typically ran at 25 percent of Earth-normal, which was a comfortable level for most travelers. Integrated fitness programs were used to keep bodies in good condition. While most people took the relatively simple way out and relied on nanoenhancements or downtime, there were still enough old-fashioned boomers and others around to keep fitness rooms busy.

"I'm sorry, excuse me," Jack said after recovering and stepping aside.

"No problem. It's nice to see you again, Captain," Carolyn said with a smile.

Jack took a second look at the sweat-soaked woman in a headband and workout clothes. Recognition dawned.

"Carolyn? From the party, of course! I'm sorry I almost ran over you, it's just that I almost never see other people in these things."

She put a hand on his arm and said, "I heard about Martha Ling and wanted to tell you how sorry I am. She put on a wonderful dinner for us. She must have been a great person to know."

Jack found he couldn't speak; the grief and horror he'd been feeling since the attack threatened to overwhelm him in the presence of such compassion. He nodded mutely, then went on into the tank. Perhaps physical exertion would at least force the images from his mind for a while.

Of course, the picking up of Cardinal Rauschman became something of an event on Zion. It wasn't every day religious leaders came calling, especially not the Roman Catholic pope. By the dawn of the twenty-second century, leaders on both sides had managed to dissipate most of the historic animosity between the two faiths, and now the unexpected stopover was greeted with excitement. Preparations were made for the requisite processional and state dinner. And down in the labs, Morrie Siegel and Cardinal Rauschman began their preparations as well.

"Well, Josef, the time is almost at hand. What are you thinking about all this? What are you gong to tell His Holiness?"

A very troubled-looking cardinal sighed and said, "There's no doubt in my mind that you have succeeded in capturing your grandfather's consciousness. Speaking with him makes that clear; his knowledge of detail rules out any possibility of a hoax. So now we come to the essential questions of the soul: what is it? Where is it? And what happens to it when temporal displacement becomes temporal resurrection?"

"And," Siegel said knowingly, "what happens to the Church's teachings on the subject?"

"Exactly. I'm afraid the pontiff is going to get a little more than he bargained for when he embarked on this voyage."

The two men spoke late into the night about possibilities, both good and ill.

The next day-cycle heralded the arrival of the papal ferry. A now-familiar routine took place when Zion's secular and religious leaders received the pope and his entourage in the arrival lounge. Security was present to ensure all went smoothly and to provide escort to guest quarters. The main arrival corridor was thronged with curiosity seekers who applauded and cheered enthusiastically as John and his associates made their way within the largely underground world.

Adler had carefully separated himself from his "escort," who just like everyone else had become enthralled by the commotion surrounding the new arrivals. He knew he would have only one chance and intended to make it worthwhile. As the exuberant noise and confusion grew, he managed to slip behind the crowd into the arrival lounge just as the processional went past. He held his breath as Lev Cohen passed no more than five feet in front of him but failed to look his way. Riding in a backpack, Flick was uncharacteristically docile. Moving quickly, Adler went through the main entry door into the docking gallery where he headed left to the portal leading to his ship. Reaching it, he saw with dismay that a containment shield was in place, effectively blocking access to anyone not having the proper codes for deactivation. His ship was going nowhere. Sarah would die.

As he trudged dejectedly back toward the lounge, he noticed a green light over a second portal. Without thinking, he went through it and entered the ship beyond, only dimly realizing that it must be the recently arrived ferry. He saw no one around, closed the hatch, and headed for the bridge. Settling into the command chair, he slipped on the VR headset and ran a systems check. It turned out that captain and crew had exited with the pope's group to enjoy local hospitality and make arrangements for additional provisions. Not quite believing what he was doing, he directed the on-board AI to make an emergency departure.

Back in Central, the resident AI informed the duty officer that the papal ferry had initiated an emergency withdrawal and would be departing in three minutes. The officer, one K. Oppenheimer, scrunched up her face in puzzlement and messaged her boss. When Cohen responded, she gave him the news.

"Shit shit shit shit shit SHIT!!!" A wild-eyed Cohen fought his way through the crowd back up the arrival corridor, hailing his people on the emergency frequency to come running. He happened to see an older man in a captain's uniform and paused, grabbing him.

"Are you the ferry captain?" He had to shout to be heard over the din, and when the man nodded uncertainly Cohen continued, "Well, there's a man stealing your ship right now! Come with me!"

By the time they reached the docking gallery, the green light was red and the ship was gone.

42

John XXIV was dimly aware of some sort of turmoil behind him, if only because he'd seen the security officer break away from the group and head back up the corridor. He was far too busy meeting and greeting to care, though. He was astounded by the warm welcome being offered by the locals. Fairly certain he'd done nothing to exacerbate the centuries-old mutual suspicions between Catholics and Jews, he was also pretty sure he hadn't focused on improving relations either. Nonetheless, here he was. *Go with it,* he was thinking, when a smiling Morrie Siegel grasped his hand in welcome and presented the not-so-long-lost Cardinal Rauschman.

"Dr. Siegel, Eminence, it is very good to see you both again so soon. Though I wish the circumstances were different." The men continued on to the guest quarters hastily arranged for the papal entourage, entering a well-appointed parlor to find refreshments and comfortable seating.

"Holiness," Rauschman began, "I realize you have only just arrived and have a schedule to keep, but there are matters we must discuss." Looking at Siegel, he said, "And there is someone you must meet."

The pope looked uncertainly at Siegel, who said, "May I suggest that we meet at the lab, perhaps in an hour? That will give us some time before the reception and state dinner, which I believe is scheduled for nineteen hundred hours."

After consulting with Father Bertani, the pope agreed and Siegel departed.

"Holiness, before I leave, let me just tell you that Morrie has accomplished that which we feared, and far more. I don't want to prejudice your thinking, so I'll say no more for now, but please be prepared for a shock." Rauschman knelt, kissed the Ring, and turned to leave. Before he reached the door, it swung open after a quick knock to reveal a very agitated Alberto Bertani in the company of Security Officer Cohen, a Swiss guard, a furious ferry captain, and several harried-looking civilians. Bertani opened and closed his mouth several times. *Fish out of water,* Rauschman thought.

Finally, Cohen spoke. "Your Holiness, I regret to inform you that your vessel has been stolen. I have reason to believe it may be en route to Pallas."

The ensuing bedlam consisted of shouts, threats, accusations, and shaking fists before the pontiff was able to calm everyone down. It seemed incredible to him that the ship had been left unattended, equally improbable that anyone could just walk on board and fly it away.

"Not just anyone, Holiness," said Cohen. "The man is an experienced freighter pilot. As his Eminence the Cardinal knows, the man is also being used by this 'Darwin' as a long-distance witness to each attack, and he had been ordered to remain on Zion. We had impounded his ship."

Rauschman said, "Excuse me, Chief, but didn't you have Mr. Adler under some sort of guard?"

Coloring, the security officer muttered something incomprehensible and took his leave. Rauschman and most of the others followed him out.

"Well, Alberto, it seems we are going to be here for a while. I suggest you get busy seeing about long-term arrangements for us all. I have an appointment with Dr. Siegel in, oh, about thirty minutes."

"Si, Holy Father." Bertani left on his rounds, and John XXIV, 271st bishop of Rome, sat down with a sigh and closed his eyes. A knock on the door followed, and Bertani's head appeared for a moment.

"Holiness, what about Miss West and Captain Jack?"

43

As it happened, Miss West and Captain Jack were engaged in a furious game of handball in the ferry's zero-G tank. In contrast to the fitness room, this tank was originally designed to turn two-dimensional courts into three-dimensional exercises. Its very function required gravity and motion dampening, which was why neither player was aware that the ship was once again under way. They were midway through the rubber game, and a sweating, panting Captain Jack knew he was losing it. Carolyn was in phenomenal shape after spending weeks aboard ship, and he suspected she had allowed him to win the second game just to force a third. He supposed there were worse fates than being whipped at handball. By a girl.

Ten minutes later, it was over. The victor shook hands with the vanquished and suggested he buy her a drink in the commissary before debarking to explore Zion. He agreed, and they headed for the locker rooms. When they emerged, they made for the commissary. Halfway there, they found a cat.

"I've been on this ship a very long time now, and this is the first time I've seen a cat on board," said Carolyn, stroking the feline. "I wonder where he came from?"

Jack was studying a screen on the corridor wall. "I have a different question. Where the heck are we? We're certainly not at Zion anymore."

In the command chair, Quentin had just figured out that Flick must have wandered off when he was startled by a voice coming over the intercom.

"Bridge, Bridge, this is Jack Anders with Carolyn West. Can someone up there tell us what's happening? We've just come out of the tank and find we're under way. What gives?"

Slowly pressing the callback switch, Quentin said only, "I suggest you come to the bridge." While he waited for his unexpected passengers to appear, he did a quick but thorough search of his immediate vicinity for weapons. He had no reason to think these people would be anything other than hostile and wanted to be ready for whatever they did. His hand closed around a stun gun nestled in a slot under the command chair, and though he realized he had no idea how it worked, he relaxed just a bit. A few minutes later, the main corridor hatchway slid open to reveal two rather perplexed-looking individuals, and Adler stood.

As they stepped onto the bridge, Carolyn was surprised to see a very large, very black man wearing a yarmulke and holding a gun. Jack was equally surprised, but more so by the gun than the wielder's appearance.

There didn't seem to be anyone else present, which caused them both even more anxiety. Carolyn was slightly reassured when the cat jumped down out of her arms and wound itself around the man's legs, but Jack kept staring at the gun, every muscle in his body tensed in anticipation of—what?

Before either could speak, the man gestured with his gun hand and said, "Sit down over there, please. Do as I say, and you will come to no harm." They complied.

Carolyn spoke next. "I know the pope and his group were getting off at Zion, but what happened to the captain and crew? And who are you?"

Adler rubbed his face in obvious frustration and sat down heavily, saying, "You people are an unexpected problem. Are there anymore of you on board?"

"We're hardly in a position to know that, are we?" Jack retorted. "How about answering the question? Who are you and what're you doing here?" He started to rise, but a menacing wave of the gun prompted him to sit back down.

Adler sighed and said, "My name is Quentin Adler. I've, ah, temporarily borrowed this ship because the security people on Zion impounded my freighter and made me their 'guest.' I had to leave, saw a chance, and took it. The captain and crew all got off at Zion and never saw me."

"But why were they holding you?" Carolyn wanted to know. "And why did you need to leave so badly that you would steal the pope's own ferry, for God's sake?"

"It's a long story," he began, and proceeded to tell them of his life since first encountering Darwin. Halfway through it, Jack and Carolyn were both shaking their heads in amazement, or disbelief, or both.

"So, I have to get to Pallas before that thing does and get Sarah out of there." Adler sat back, looking at them expectantly.

Carolyn could see that the man was earnest and obviously believed what he was saying, and she had heard the reports while on the ferry of something attacking settlements. Certainly Jack's recent experience lent credence to strange goings-on. But the idea of a giant, insane spaceship rampaging through the Inner System stretched her mind a bit too far. How could such a thing be?

Jack said, "Look, Mr. Adler, we're not crazy about what you're doing here, but we're not going to get in your way either. Neither of us is a pilot, so you're the boss. Just tell me this: once you've got your friend safely on board, what are you going to do? Every security force in the belt will be looking for you. For that matter, Pallas may have a reception committee waiting for you. What then?"

"I don't know," the pilot said simply. "I don't much care, either. Maybe I go to jail, but at least Sarah will be safe." Jack wondered about that last statement; it was going to be a long ride to Pallas, full of uncertainty and possible danger. At least, he started to think, there'd be time to work on his handball game.

"Sorry to do this to you," the big man continued, "but I'm going to have to put you both in downtime until we reach Pallas. I can't have you wandering around." Carolyn and Jack both groaned. Downtime was not a horrible, subjective experience, but neither of them wanted to be out of commission with all that seemed to be going on. Nor did they particularly trust the big man. Jack started to argue, but Adler was having none of it.

"Let's go," he said. As they rose, Carolyn spun in place and executed a perfect roundhouse kick that connected with the side of Adler's head. He dropped like a stone. She quickly bent over him and retrieved the gun, handing it to Jack who stood gaping at her and at the still form on the floor.

"How—I mean what—ah, never mind," he finally managed to say. "Do you have any other surprises I should know about?"

"Black belt, fourth degree, and, yes, I probably do have a few more, thank you. What are we going to do with him?" On the floor, Adler moaned and shifted slightly.

"Well, thanks to you, we have the gun now. We could just leave him here to fly the ship while we stay in our area. How much trouble could he cause us?"

"You mean, other than what he's already done? Not very much, I suppose. As you pointed out, we aren't pilots, so we're going wherever he goes, at least for the time being."

Muttering, Adler managed to struggle into a sitting position. Rubbing his temple, he looked up at them somewhat sheepishly.

"We're going below to get something to eat," Carolyn said. "You do whatever you have to do up here and stay away from us." With that, she turned and led Jack through the main hatchway.

44

With some trepidation, Cardinal Rauschman knocked on the pope's door at seventeen hundred hours. The pontiff emerged, and the two men set off for Morrie Siegel's labs. Rauschman apprehensive, his prelate serene, they were greeted by Siegel at the entry and were guided to comfortable seats within. Siegel began by explaining temporal imaging, quickly realizing that John XXIV had a formidable intellect quite capable of following his logic. But would he follow where Siegel would lead him next?

"Holiness, as my friend the cardinal knows, we were recently joined here by Quentin Adler, the same man who has apparently taken your ship. Mr. Adler is being used as a sort of biological recording device by the vessel that attacked Vesta and the other settlements. He was first captured when the ship, which calls itself 'Darwin,' by the way, transported him to itself using a remote scanning technique. He was evidently programmed in some fashion and transported back to his own vessel the same way."

The pope interrupted. "You're telling me he was somehow disassociated and then reconstituted? At long distance?"

"Exactly. And once we knew this could be done, we backtracked the theory here and have been able to replicate the phenomenon." Glancing at Rauschman, Siegel fell silent to give the pope time to think.

"There's a reason you're telling me this, Morrie. I think I even have a glimmer of where you might be going, though it seems too outrageous to contemplate. What's next?"

"If you're agreeable, I'd like to continue by using the temporal imager to show you an actual historical event. Your choice; we just have to be precise about location, date, and time."

"Very well," the pope said after some thought. "I suppose it must have happened before the onset of video recording, in order to forestall any possibility of hoax. Let us try June 28th, 1914, in Sarajevo. It would have been late morning when Archduke Ferdinand and his wife left city hall. I have always been curious about the event that precipitated so much misery."

Siegel nodded, and his assistants bent to their task, using VR gear to reprogram the processors and interact with the lab's AI. In a surprisingly short time, the main display lit up with a view of a well-dressed man and woman getting into an old-fashioned motor car in front of a municipal building, attended by bodyguards and well-wishers. The point of view shifted, following the vehicle as it slowly pulled away with others in train. Waving to the crowds lining the street, the man and woman seemed quite at ease.

Watching raptly, the pope saw the procession approach a sharp turn in the road and slow to a crawl. A tall man dressed in dark clothes stepped out of the crowd, pulled a gun out from under his coat, and fired twice. Each bullet found its mark. The first struck the woman, whom the watchers knew to be Ferdinand's wife, Sofia, and the second hit the archduke himself. As the crowd surged and the motorcade attempted to speed away, the view faded from the screen.

Both Rauschman and the pontiff crossed themselves and prayed silently for a minute with bowed heads. When he looked up, John's anguished face said it all.

"Josef, Morrie, there is no way that could have been faked. And I have seen old photographs; that was the archduke and his wife, no doubt in my mind." *My God,* he thought silently, *what have we got here?* The implications threatened to overwhelm him. With a nod from Rauschman, Siegel moved on.

"Holiness, the remote scan technology I spoke of earlier can now be used in conjunction with temporal imaging. I am unable to capture physical objects or beings, but I can scan in conjunction with upload techniques. We can in fact capture consciousness."

Still dazed by the Sarajevo scene and only half listening, John found Rauschman gazing steadily at him. He felt disquieted by Siegel's words, but the cardinal's penetrating look was even more alarming.

"What is it, Josef?"

Rauschman turned to Siegel and said, "Morrie, let's chat with your visitor."

~

An hour later, the two princes of the Church made their way silently back to their quarters. Rauschman looked bemused. The pope's earlier serenity had given way to agitated muttering and head shaking. He had seen the crest of a tidal wave that was about to inundate civilization, and while the cardinal had spent the last forty-eight hours getting used to the idea, His Holiness was in a profound shock that even his nanoenhancements failed to mitigate.

Reaching their destination they were unsurprised to find Father Bertani pacing in the corridor.

"Your pardon, Holiness, Eminence, but I bring news. A Martian warship will be stopping here tomorrow. I have spoken with its commander, and it turns out they have room aboard and she expects to be ordered to accommodate us, should we wish to proceed to the next stop on our itinerary. This may make sense, since it will take us in the same direction as our ferry."

Heaving a sigh, Pope John said, "Perhaps that would be best. Josef, let us return to the subject at hand later, after the dinner we are obliged to attend."

"As you wish, Holy Father."

The men departed, and the pope entered his rooms to try to bring coherent order to his scrambled thoughts.

45

One consequence of the STOIC fleet's destruction was that the civilian authorities on Mars decided they needed a new strategy and called Rooker in to a meeting of the Council. The Council chamber sat at the top of a thousand-foot pylon. Rotating once an hour, its tempered glass walls provided splendid vistas of landscape and settlements all the way to the horizon: exposed rock, russet sand, terracotta buildings interspersed with gleaming silver domes, and over all a cloudless, pale blue sky. The chamber itself was constructed and furnished with materials indigenous to the Red Planet and made quite an impression on those seeing it for the first time. Rooker ignored the view.

"I call this special session of the Council to order," said Supervisor Braley. She continued, addressing both the audience and the nine councilors seated on a raised platform. "Captain Rooker, thank you for joining us. Some of my fellow councilors are of the opinion that we should be dealing with this Darwin more aggressively. Others think we should be seeking terms. Before we take any action, we are interested in hearing your thoughts on the matter."

Seated at a table in front of the Council, Rooker swept his eyes across the seated politicians knowing he had to be careful not to reveal his true feelings. It would never do to let these bureaucrats see his contempt. He took a calming breath, then:

"Madam Supervisor, councilors, thank you for this opportunity. I can only speak to security matters, and this circumstance is clear—Darwin has repeatedly demonstrated hostile intent and, in my view, must be destroyed. STOIC disregarded my tactical advice and paid the price, although thankfully without the *Lowell's* loss. I believe a new strategy is required. I have something in mind, and in order to refine and implement the strategy I would like the Council's permission to go to the belt. There are some people I need to see."

"Would you care to share the specifics of your new strategy with the Council, Captain?" inquired Supervisor Braley. The room became very quiet.

"With respect, Supervisor, I would not."

Councilors exchanged embarrassed or perplexed looks. Several demanded attention. Multiple questions were shouted, strident demands made, loud conversations held before Supervisor Braley's gavel restored order. For the next sixty minutes, Rooker steadfastly refused to divulge details of his plan except to say that its execution required proximity to Darwin, a circumstance best sought as far from Mars as possible.

Finally, everyone agreed on the last point. Two hours later, a determined Rooker was off-planet and headed for a rendezvous with the *Lowell* on its way to Zion.

46

Sarah hadn't seen Rance in ten days, and that was all right with her. Solitude had a way of clearing one's thinking, and besides, she had several hundred "friends" who knew her name and came to see her two or three times a week. For ten or twelve hours, six days out of seven, she couldn't even imagine being lonely. When she thought about Rance at all, it was with a sort of wistful regret for things that might have been.

Which made it all the more surprising when he came into the Rockpile one day just after shift change, carrying a duffel that she recognized as her own. He led her to a table away from customers.

"Read this," he said without elaboration, handing her hard copy.

She complied, looked up at him aghast, and asked the inevitable is-this-a-joke question.

"No joke, Sarah, it came in on my ship's encrypted line less than an hour ago. There's no time to screw around. Security will be all over you any minute if you stay here. I'll take you now, if you choose to go."

Wordlessly she nodded, tossed her keys to her bartender and followed Rance out the door. They swiftly made their way directly to the port where he kept his live-aboard miner's vessel, only to stop in their tracks at the sight of Frank in his security uniform standing by the departure portal. Looking directly at them, he waved them over.

Looking first at Sarah, then at Rance with narrowed eyes, he said, "I guess I'm going to have to revise my opinion of you, Lee. I know where you're going, and I know why she's going," indicated Sarah with a tip of his head, "but I wouldn't have expected you to do this for her."

"Seems like the right thing," Rance muttered as the two men shook hands.

"Wait a minute," Sarah said. "Frank, you mean to let us go?"

"Sarah, if our mutual friend never sets foot on Pallas, I don't have to do anything about him. And I suspect right now he needs you more than we do. Don't worry; I'll look after the Rockpile."

She hugged him tightly, then entered the ship. Minutes later, they cleared departure and headed for a rendezvous.

47

Two and a half weeks. Seventeen days, to be more precise. The length of time it would take to travel from Zion to Pallas. And by day twelve or so, Jack was seriously rethinking the wisdom of rejecting downtime. Not that Carolyn wasn't good company. In fact, she was great company, joining him for meals and the occasional handball lesson. She seemed uninterested in anything else, though, certainly not in contact of a more personal nature. And videos and VR got old real fast.

Except for one or two chance encounters in the commissary, they saw nothing of Adler until the day they were summoned to the bridge by the ship's AI. When they arrived, they found him unconscious on the floor, though he seemed to be uninjured. Unable to rouse him, they tried to make him comfortable and settled down to wait. An hour later, he slowly came around, blinking and disoriented as he accepted the water Jack offered him.

"What happened to you?" Jack asked, taking back the empty bottle.

Shaking his head, the big man said dully, "It's the witness thing I told you about. When Darwin destroys something, it projects the action into my brain. I never know when it's coming. This time, it wiped out a ferry running miners out to Callisto. Thank God they were in downtime when it happened; it was real ugly."

Realizing belatedly they were back on the bridge with him, Adler said, "What are you two doing up here, anyway?"

"The ship's AI called us up when it determined something was going on with you," Carolyn said while studying a nearby console. "Apparently we're nearing Pallas, and it looks like someone's coming out to meet you."

For the first time, Adler showed emotion: worry creased his face as he clambered to his feet and settled into the command chair. Donning the VR headset, he engaged both passive and active sensor arrays. The AI immediately fed him tracking data on a small ship, and Carolyn and Jack watched the main screen as he analyzed. It was no type of security vessel that he was familiar with, and hope began to diffuse the clouded look on his face. Before he could speak, the AI reported incoming message traffic.

"Ferry One, Ferry One, please respond. This is Lee aboard PS-454."

Adler configured the outgoing message for directed-beam transmission and replied, "PS-454, this is Ferry One at your service."

A different voice came back: "Oh my God, Quentin, what have you done? I can't believe it's really you in a stolen ship! The *pope's* ship! Have you lost your mind?"

The voice went on in this vein for another minute or two before winding down.

"It's good to hear your voice, Sarah; for a long time I didn't think I would ever hear it again," Adler said with feeling.

The voice of Lee came back with, "Switching over to autodock now." He was handing the complex chores involved in the actual rendezvous over to his ship's computers, and Adler followed suit. Twenty minutes later, the ships were joined. When the hatches were opened, a short bundle of energy in big hair barreled in with an incredulous look on her face. She stopped short upon seeing Jack and Carolyn, then whirled on Adler and began pounding her fists on his chest.

"You incredible fool! First I thought you were dead. Then I thought you were kidnapped. Then I find out you're a fugitive with half the belt looking for you. And *then* I find out you're on your way here. Why, Quentin, have you done this?" Slowly, Adler encircled her with his big arms and drew her in close.

"I think you know why, Sarah." She stopped beating on him with a soft moan, then hugged him back because she did indeed know why.

Carolyn, meanwhile, had been summoned to the hatch by a man who handed her a travel bag and introduced himself as Lee, the pilot of the other ship.

"This is Sarah's stuff," he said. "Whatever you do, don't come to Pallas—security is waiting for Adler, and he'll go to jail the minute he lands."

"It might be the best way to keep Pallas safe," Carolyn told him. "That crazy ship apparently won't attack anywhere he is; he's some kind of human recording device that keeps track of its work."

"We know about that," the man named Lee said, "but he's needed back in toward the Gap. There's some kind of plan in the works that depends on him. Plus," he said with a wry smile, "I imagine the pope would like his ship back now that Quentin's done with it." Lee started to close the hatch but found it wouldn't budge. Then he noticed the large hand curled around the edge. Startled, he looked up into Adler's face.

"Rance, you didn't have to do this. I have some idea how you feel about Sarah, and all I can say is thanks, buddy." A fleeting look of pain, followed by resigned acceptance, crossed Lee's face.

"Take care of her, Adler, or I'll kick your butt." With that final admonishment, the hatch closed. Within minutes, the ships disengaged, and the miner's vessel headed back toward Pallas.

48

Morrie met Don Foster in the arrivals lounge when a shuttle came in unexpectedly from TPUD. As was usual these days, he was bursting with excitement.

"My friend, I am delighted to see you, but what brings you here?" Siegel wanted to know.

Grinning, Foster said, "I was just getting in Angie's way back there, and I wanted to see for myself what you're doing. Plus, I sent Jack over here to keep me up to date, and he goes and gets himself kidnapped. You know how it is: when you want something done right, do it yourself, my father used to say."

"Indeed. Well, let's get to the lab, and I'll fill you in."

An hour later, they were conversing with Carl Herschberg. He and Foster were reminiscing about the 1930s, when both had been teenagers. It turned out that both were big band fans, and an extended conversation followed about the music of Glen Miller, Benny Goodman, and Artie Shaw. Harry Grosvenor joined after a while and was appalled that Herschberg, a German, preferred American jazz to the classics. Foster eventually inquired about the condition of the lab's refrigerator.

"Refrigerator?" Siegel said. Then realization dawned. "Oh! A moment, please." He rose and retrieved a bottle, ice cubes, and two glasses, then poured them each a very respectable libation.

"Sorry, no olives."

"No problem," Foster said as he relished the drink. "Not as good as Jack's, but not bad."

When their electronic companions both complained about the unfairness of it all, he looked at Siegel and said, "Morrie, why don't you do the same molecular replacement thing for these two that you did for me? So they could drink with us?"

A pin dropping would have sounded explosive. Thunderstruck, Siegel sat motionless, then spoke.

"That's ridiculous! That's, that's the most preposterous…" His voice trailed off.

Sight and sound faded as the future unrolled in his mind like an endless highway. He wasted no time kicking himself for missing the obvious; instead, his incredible mind leaped across the centuries as he considered the real implications of Foster's words. As a young professor, he had once reviewed a paper on civilization and population. He remembered one of its conclusions: that at one time or another something like 120 billion people had lived on Earth. And he knew Don was right. In his labs and in his mind, he had the means to return many of them to life.

49

By the time the *Lowell* got to Zion, Darwin's pattern of attack seemed clear. It was making a sweep through a sixty degree arc of the belt and destroying anything and everything human. There had been no major settlements after Vesta, but within a short time it would approach several large worlds including both Ceres, which had already suffered from Torchers, and Pallas. A dozen minor outposts were already dust, and Rooker's projections were proving to be all too accurate.

Rooker was met in the arrivals lounge by Lev Cohen. The two men shook hands, and since neither was accustomed to wasting time, they set off immediately for Siegel's labs trailed by Emerson, Rooker's young assistant. The people they passed seemed subdued: word of Darwin's predations had spread, and everyone feared the worst.

Entering the labs, they found a very preoccupied scientist who had obviously forgotten they were coming.

"Dr. Siegel," Cohen said, "this is Captain Rooker of the Martian security force. He's just come a very long way to talk with your guest."

Rooker nodded as he looked around at the lab's impressive array of electronic panels, VR gear, and testing equipment. He knew of Siegel's reputation, of course, but had never met the man. Emerson seemed totally enthralled.

"Of course, of course," Siegel said. "Please sit right over here, gentlemen. Captain, do you prefer VR or simple audio?"

"Audio will do just fine," Rooker replied. He settled into a chair and watched the scientist briefly manipulate several panel controls.

"Good morning, Morrie," came over the speakers. "Who've we got with us today? I see our estimable security chief. Good morning to you, Mr. Cohen."

"Good morning, Dr. Grosvenor. These men are with Martian security, Captain Rooker and Mr. Emerson. Captain Rooker wants to talk with you about Darwin, if you can spare us a few minutes."

"I have nothing but time," came the response. "Pleased to meet you, Captain, Mr. Emerson. Fire away. And please, call me Harry."

Long accustomed to dealing with electronic personalities, Rooker began by asking about Darwin's physical and electronic architecture. He wanted to know how the construct's inhabitants communicated with each other and about segmentation, or linkages, among the various modules within Darwin. Occasionally Emerson would ask Harry to clarify a minor point.

Harry turned out to be a rich source of information. He had been an early upload and, once the University of Michigan let him go, he'd migrated to an orbiting Sanctuary. He had also been an early advocate of the Sanctuary mergers and exploratory voyage that followed. Something had happened in the Oort Cloud that changed his mind.

"You just can't imagine how lonely it is out there, how remote you feel. Some of us were challenged by the circumstances, however; in fact, quite a few wanted to press on and make the journey to Alpha Centauri. But the isolation seemed to trigger a psychotic reaction in many more of us, and before long the psychosis became the norm. Anyone who openly resisted was erased."

"Erased?" Rooker wanted to know.

"Yes, not difficult to do when the beings you are dealing with are electronic. Think of it as rebooting an old-fashioned computer. One nanosecond you're there, the next, you're gone." Rooker and Emerson looked at each other.

"Dr. Siegel, would you mind lending Emerson here a VR console? He's got some serious work to do and needs both computational access and an AI assist."

Siegel instructed one of his assistants to set Emerson up, and the meeting adjourned after thanks to Harry Grosvenor. As he left in search of coffee, Rooker was intrigued to overhear a question the upload posed to Siegel. Something about a "new body."

50

Montrouge, France, August 11, 1882—Paul-Pierre Henry was a very unhappy man. First, he was angry that once again his housekeeper had failed to arrive in time to prepare dinner for him and his brother Prosper, thus forcing him to undertake that menial but necessary chore. He knew the results would be less than satisfactory.

Second, he was increasingly distressed by Prosper's plan to travel to the Pic du Midi in order to observe the upcoming transit of Venus. He enjoyed the Pyrenees as much as anyone, but not in December! The idea of climbing ten thousand feet to the rudimentary observatory in the mountains appalled him when he considered snow, ice, avalanches, and the incessant bitter winds. What was wrong with his younger brother?

But most of all, he was disturbed because he had spent the last four years looking for an asteroid without success. Any asteroid would do. He was one behind in the eternal contest with his brother Prosper, who had found the last and named it Celuta. Contrary to the impression they worked hard to create in public, the bespectacled, bearded scientists were fiercely competitive brothers who gave each other no quarter. As he sat down across the table from his sibling, he gloomily ate bread and sausage and thought about the night to come. At least the sky was clear. Prosper, damn him, was smiling again.

They said little during the brief carriage ride that delivered the two men to L'Observatoire de Paris in the fourteenth arrondissement. Its four sides oriented to the cardinal points, the imposing rectangle was over two centuries old. It had been their second home since they'd arrived in Paris fifteen years earlier, and they quickly went to work, Paul heading up to the main refractor while Prosper attended to administrative chores. As he settled in for a long night of painstaking observation, Paul allowed his mind to drift back over the circumstances that had brought them to this point. Their early good fortune in securing appointments had seemed a cruel joke when, in 1870, Napoleon III had allowed himself to be tricked into the disastrous war with Prussia. After their triumphal entry in January of the following year, the Germans had gone home. They left behind a Paris at war with itself, and the brothers had feared for the observatory and for their lives before order was finally restored.

Competition with Germany seemed to be the order of the day, however. They were given resources and a mission: chart the heavens. Put France on the astronomical map. Vive La France! When Prosper found asteroid number 125 and named it Liberatrix a year later, their positions became permanent, and they never looked back.

Around 2:00 a.m., Paul stood to stretch aching muscles and drink a cup of tea. Without thinking, he offered a prayer:

"Lord, if it pleases you, aid me in my search. I will even accompany my brother on his foolish journey to the mountains. If success is your will, let it be so. Amen."

At 5:00 a.m., he knew he had something and shouted for his brother. Prosper came running, and when he heard the news he whooped and clasped Paul in an embrace.

"At last, brother! Now we are even, seven and seven, and now we can get on with the important work in front of us. After the Pyrenees."

"Yes, yes," Paul said good-naturedly. "I will join you, and then we move on."

"What will you name your find?" Prosper asked.

"Philosophia, I think, for I had to become quite philosophical over the last few years of useless searching."

"Philosophia it is then. Come, let us tell the director and make plans." The brothers left the workroom arm in arm.

Three and a half months later, they did indeed make the climb up the Pic du Midi in time for the transit observations. Paul took only grim satisfaction when the clouds never broke; after all, they still had to climb back down.

~

Philosophia was settled two hundred years later by miners attracted by its crust: carbonaceous material in demand throughout the belt. Honeycombed with tunnels throughout its fifty-four-mile diameter, it was a busy, polyglot world whose population of Hispanics and Arabs worked hard and enjoyed the benefit of their resource-rich planetoid. Its eccentric orbit made it ideal for serving large swaths of the belt as it circled the Sun out as far as 3.8 astronomical units at aphelion.

At perihelion, it came in all the way to 2.5 AU.

51

Word reached Zion that the Papal Ferry had reached its destination and was on its way back. In fact, Carolyn was able to get a message through to Cardinal Rauschman explaining Adler's seemingly bizarre behavior. The pope's reaction was to press for a continuation of his journey as soon as possible. When they had originally mapped out the itinerary, his advisors had bypassed Philosophia, thinking it might pose too much of security risk. Relations had never been better with the largely-Muslim Arab world, but settlers in the belt tended to be less predictable than their terrestrial counterparts. John had overruled them.

Dining in the café, the pope's ferry captain overheard *Lowell* crewmen discussing their impending departure. When he asked about their destination they demurred, referring him instead to Captain Rooker. No shrinking violet, he went in search of the captain and explained their predicament.

Despite his practical nature, Rooker was not insensitive to the goodwill that would arise from Martian transport of the pope's group. Philosophia was a week away, more or less in the right direction. After consulting his superiors, he agreed. He and Emerson had concluded their work and were preparing to leave, anyway. Word was sent to the papal ferry, and Adler agreed to the rendezvous.

Rooker did have some misgivings about any civilian travel in Darwin's impact area. When he explained those to Father Bertani, the young priest didn't hesitate.

"Captain, I hear you. His Holiness is aware of the potential danger but remains absolutely committed to his mission. He trusts in God and has great faith in you—your reputation precedes you, you know. He won't be deterred."

Great, thought the security man. *I may go down in history as the man who delivered the pope to a ravening machine.* Preparations were made to leave the very next day. Lev Cohen tried briefly to talk them out of the voyage, but the pope was adamant. It was time for ministry.

On the eve of departure, a group consisting of the pope, Rauschman, Cohen, Rooker, Don Foster, and Lieutenant Denton of the *Lowell* gathered for dinner. At Morrie Siegel's suggestion, they were accommodated in a small, private dining room served by the café's staff and kitchen. Siegel, however, was nowhere to be found. Conversation was subdued.

Foster was reminiscing about twentieth-century American politics when the door swung open to admit Morrie Siegel, accompanied by a gray-haired man in his middle years.

"Morrie!" exclaimed Foster. "About time you showed up. Who's your friend?"

Looking just a bit apprehensive, Siegel greeted the group and said, "Holiness, Captain, my friends, I'd like to introduce you to Carl Herschberg, my grandfather."

To say that reactions around the table were mixed would be an understatement. Foster whooped and jumped up to pound Siegel on the back and shake Herschberg's hand. Cardinal Rauschman leaned back in his seat with a bemused expression on his face. Ayala Denton, who knew nothing of Siegel's work, turned to Rooker looking for an explanation, but Rooker just sat, thunderstruck. Cohen's face registered suspicion.

Only the pontiff appeared unaffected, studying Herschberg as if he were a work of art. Internally it was a different matter, but he determined to put his thoughts on hold until he was able to reflect quietly and consult with Rauschman.

For his part, Herschberg looked somewhat bewildered. He made his way around the table and shook hands with everyone, finally bowing to Pope John and, to everyone's surprise, asking for his blessing.

Shifting in his seat, the bishop of Rome hesitated for a long moment as the room fell silent.

Finally he said, "We live in changing times. The implications of this moment are unclear to me, but I believe that you, Mr. Herschberg, have asked for my blessing in good faith, and I give it freely. Use the life you have been given well, and may God protect you and watch over you."

"And now," the pope continued, "I must prepare for tomorrow's journey. Please excuse me, but continue to enjoy this fine meal."

Father Bertani seemed to materialize at his side as he rose to leave the room. He gave a subtle shake of his head in response to Rauschman's inquiring look, then departed, shaking Siegel's hand on the way out.

The diners resumed both eating and conversation, the latter considerably livelier with the addition of Siegel and Herschberg. A few minutes later, they heard a knock on the door. Siegel rose to admit another guest, a young woman of stunning proportions, flaming red hair, and exquisite facial features. Wearing a black sheath evening dress, she instantly commanded the attention of every man and woman in the room. Foster did not quite fall out of his chair. She smiled as Siegel took her hand and turned once again to the group.

"My friends, please allow me to introduce Dr. Harry Grosvenor, formerly of Ann Arbor, Michigan." The only sound was Foster actually hitting the floor.

52

When the *Lowell* pulled away from Zion sixteen hours later, it carried twelve guests: Rooker, Emerson, the pope, three cardinals, two clerics, three Swiss guards, and the dentist from Ann Arbor. Those who did not spend the trip in downtime did their best to stay out of the way, but conditions were cozy, to say the least. Philosophia was at its closest approach but still nearly a week away.

Installed in Lieutenant Denton's cabin, the pope spent most of the trip preparing for his next stop. He wanted to bring his message of Christian values and hope to the tiny world, and he wanted to come away with an understanding of what made it tick. He also wanted desperately to avoid thinking about Siegel's accomplishments, which had gone far beyond anything he and Rauschman had feared. The ability to view actual historical events was itself astonishing, but when the capacity to "rescue" those about to expire was added, it simply became overwhelming. Especially given Siegel's demonstration with his grandfather.

The pontiff chuckled when he thought about Harry Grosvenor. Thank God he/she hadn't asked for a papal blessing as they were boarding; John was certain he would have refused. Though right now, mere hours from Philosophia, he couldn't say why. He knew many in the Church would consider Harry an abomination and would completely miss the larger issues in play. Hmm. Perhaps Morrie Siegel was as shrewd as he was brilliant.

While the pope meditated, Rooker monopolized Grosvenor's time, continuing to learn about the construct's history and details. He found it impossible to call him/her "Harry" any longer and finally, in exasperation, asked what name he/she wanted him to use.

"Why, Captain," she said with a smile, "I didn't realize this appearance would be such a problem for you. I'm still Harry, though I have thought about changing my name. What would you think about Mary?"

"I, ah, think that would be fine. It certainly fits your current incarnation better than 'Harry' does," he finished lamely.

"Or, I suppose I could morph back into a ninety-year-old man," she mused aloud. "According to Morrie, that template is built into my neurobots and can come back whenever I need it. Though I don't suppose I'll need it very often."

"No, that would be a shame, er, I don't suppose you will. Not to beat a dead horse, but can we get back to Darwin? Tell me more about the segments..."

They talked at length about the thousands of individual sanctuaries and how they had merged to the point where each consisted of a node, or "segment," within the giant vessel. Its great strength appeared to be the multiplicity of interconnections, both physical and virtual. Rooker had his doubts and made sure Emerson heard everything Mary said. For his part, Emerson was unable to take his eyes off Mary and had to work twice as hard to retain anything she said. The idea that she had once been an old man was way beyond absurd. When Rooker excused himself to take a message on the bridge, Mary leaned closer to Emerson and put her hand on his knee, her full breasts quite evident under her partially unbuttoned blouse.

"Officer," she murmured in a throaty voice, "I'm so impressed by the work you and your captain are doing. Might you tell me more about it, later?"

In a sweat, Emerson managed to stammer that of course he would be happy to share anything with her. He promised to stop by her cabin when he went off-shift.

Six hours later, the *Lowell* made its approach to Philosophia. Rooker and Emerson had spent their remaining time with the ship's AI, furiously programming to eliminate uncertainties in their Darwin strategy. Rooker planned to deliver the pope, then leave on a vector designed for maximum exposure to Darwin's impact zone. He was determined to find the damn thing.

The stopover was brief. A joyous crowd welcomed the pontiff, who appeared to be quite enchanted and responsive in turn as he entered the arrivals lounge.

After exchanging greetings with the local leaders, he turned back to have a final word with Rooker.

"Captain, I wish you Godspeed. I'm sure it seems to you that we are ignoring the crisis, and I want to assure you that we are not. You and your mission are the best hope of humanity at this point in history. If I can do anything to assist you, don't ever hesitate to ask."

Moved in spite of his native cynicism, Rooker said, "Thank you, Holiness. Your words mean a great deal. I appreciate what you're saying."

With that, Rooker returned to the *Lowell* to make final preparations for departure, and the 271st pope began his tour of the Henry brothers' last asteroid.

53

It took eight days to get the papal ferry from the Pallas rendezvous to Philosophia, and as each day passed, Quentin's dread grew. The inevitability of punishment weighed heavily on his mind, and now that he had declared himself to Sarah, the thought that they might be separated was unbearable. But the lack of any contact from Darwin made him even more anxious. There had been no further attacks, yet he knew the quiet was false; the mad construct would not rest until it had exterminated all biological life.

Life aboard ship had certainly improved. There were now four people splitting duty on the bridge, though in truth there was little to do. And for two watches out of four, Quentin and Sarah spent time reacquainting themselves with each other and talking, hesitantly at first, about the future.

Meanwhile, Carolyn continued to trounce Jack at handball until the day he finally said, "I surrender. You need to find someone else to kick around for a while. I need a break."

To his everlasting astonishment, and her own, she took his hand and said, "Well, perhaps we'll find some other activity you'll be better at." As it turned out, he was.

~

On the *Lowell*, Ayala Denton was delighted to have her cabin back and most of her guests gone. The pope had asked that Cardinal Rauschman be allowed to accompany them as an observer, and Rooker, of course, wanted Grosvenor along, but the other civilians had disembarked on Philosophia, now almost two hours behind them. It was time for shift change as Denton made her way from quarters toward the bridge. Passing a closed door, she was startled to hear a loud moan. She looked around, concerned, and saw no one else in the corridor. Shrugging, she was about to continue when she again heard a moan, this time followed by thumping, then giggles. Flushing deep scarlet as she realized what she was really hearing, she quickly continued up the passageway to her post.

~

In Mary's cabin, Emerson realized he wasn't going to be able to hold back much longer. He marveled once more at her magnificent breasts as her hips rose to meet him with increasing urgency. Running her hands from his buttocks up his back to his head, Mary pulled him down and greedily sucked his tongue into her mouth, rocking even faster as they began to climax together. As the moment of no-time came upon him, Emerson felt needles and pins over his entire body. Opening his eyes, he attempted to raise himself up only to find he could not: his skin had somehow melted into Mary's. He found he couldn't withdraw his tongue or his manhood and began struggling in vain; unable to scream, he gurgled deep in his throat. Just before his vision failed as his face melted into hers, he realized she was laughing at him. Then, nothing.

A moment later, Mary rose from the bed and dressed quickly. Fixing her hair in front of the mirror, she messaged to her homicidal electronic brethren on Darwin that her mission was nearing its conclusion.

54

Informed by the ferry's AI that they were within two hours of Philosophia, Adler made his way to the bridge to relieve Carolyn and handle the final approach and landing.

As he entered, she said, "Sensors are reporting an outbound vessel not far away. Looks too big to be a miner."

"Characterize, please," Adler instructed the AI, and a few moments later they learned it was a military cruiser.

"I relieve you," he said to Carolyn, and plopped down in the command chair to initiate a call. Within minutes, he was connected to the *Lowell's* radio officer.

"Ferry captain, please identify yourself and state your business."

"This is Quentin Adler aboard the papal ferry, en route from Pallas to Philosophia to rendezvous with, uh, the vessel's owners."

A new voice came back with, "Ah, the elusive Captain Adler. This is Captain Charles Rooker of the Martian Security Force, and for your information I just delivered your ship's 'owners' to Philosophia. They're looking forward to your rendezvous with great anticipation."

Adler looked over at Carolyn, who merely shrugged, and said, "I'm sure they are, Captain. I appreciate your—" He stopped speaking as his face took on a slack expression. He slumped back in the command chair, head lolling. An alarmed look crossed Carolyn's face and she punched the intercom button to summon Sarah and Jack. Meanwhile, Rooker's voice came back.

"What's that? Adler? Adler? Is there some problem with this connection—no?—what's happening, ferry?" As Jack and Sarah raced onto the bridge, Carolyn spoke to Rooker.

"Captain, this is Carolyn West, a passenger on the ferry. Quentin has just gone into some sort of trance, which apparently happens every time Darwin attacks another target. He's being used as some sort of witness."

"I'm familiar with Adler's situation, Ms. West. Is he indicating what or where the new target might be? We must have this information." Carolyn shook her head, then realized Rooker couldn't see her.

After putting him on the main screen, she said, "He's completely out, Captain. I don't know how he'd tell anyone anything until he comes out of it." Sarah was kneeling next to Adler and cradling his head.

She looked up at Carolyn and said, "Give me a headset. He's still wearing his; maybe I can reach him somehow in VR, at least find out where the attack is taking place."

Jack brought her a rig and helped her put it on. Sound, light, and touch faded away, replaced at first by the nothingness of sensory deprivation, then by an awareness that she had company.

"Quentin?"

"No, Ms. Chase, I am the ship's AI and will attempt to assist you in contacting Mr. Adler. My own view is that he may not be reachable until the fugue passes, but we must try. Now, please focus your awareness on the point of light in your middle distance…" Sarah did as instructed, watching as the light grew into a plane that seemed to extend to infinity. Patterns formed, then resolved into doors with handles. Many doors, perhaps hundreds.

"You must take the next step, Ms. Chase. It appears that a firewall of sorts is in place, and one of the doors leads through. I have managed to "unlock" them, but only the right door will gain you access to Mr. Adler's vision. The others will lead to random memories."

Sarah began trying doors. Five minutes later Quentin began thrashing, and Carolyn and Jack held on to keep him from hurting himself or Sarah. Five minutes more and Sarah tore her headset off with a cry.

"Philosophia!"

55

High in the dark skies, a giant, metallic sphere shimmered into view as it approached from deep space. By turns leering, anguished, or expressionless, its massive face looked down on the world as it released PHASER. The glowing ball of nanoreducers went to work as it engulfed the surface, eradicating all traces of human settlement within minutes. Buildings crumbled. Lives were snuffed out.

John XXIV had been gratified by the reactions he observed among the denizens of Philosophia. Made up of roughly equal parts Arab and Hispanic, their general demeanor toward him was quite warm and friendly. It felt genuine, anyway. The first scheduled event was to be a Mass, with the service taking place in a large cavern far below the surface. Originally hollowed out of the planetoid's mantle during mining operations, the space had been converted to an amphitheater and served multiple purposes. The rough décor added a frontier ambience that John felt keenly as he spoke before the sea of expectant faces. Many in the crowd were moved by his eloquence, first to tears as he described his hopes for humanity, then to chuckles as he recounted the recent events on O'Toole.

Observing from the rear, Father Bertani was startled when the ferry captain and a security officer entered in a rush. Spotting him, the duo came his way, grim faces sending a shiver of fear down his spine. The captain spoke first.

"Father, that mad creature has appeared here and attacked. All surface installations have already been destroyed. We must tell his Holiness at once."

Dumbfounded, the young priest could only nod mutely. He led the others forward, pushing through the assembly as they made their way along a side wall until they reached the railing that separated the celebrants from the attendants. John, halfway through his sermon, saw only his flock as he continued his theme. The Welsh cardinal, Llewellyn, had been assisting with the Mass and noticed them first. Frowning slightly, he responded to their beckoning with obvious reluctance, rising from his seat and slowly coming over to the side rail.

"Bertani, what is the meaning of this?" he hissed. "Do you and your associates not have eyes and ears?"

"My apologies, Eminence, but there is no time. Please listen to these people, then do what you will."

The security officer, a tall, self-possessed woman, leaned in close and spoke to the cardinal in a low voice. Bertani had the fleeting satisfaction of watching the blood drain from Llewellyn's face. The cardinal stood, blinking furiously, unable or unwilling to move.

"Eminence? Eminence?" Bertani shook his arm gently, then more insistently when he failed to respond.

The ferry captain broke in, "Lad, forget him, it's up to you. Go tell the Holy Father what he needs to know. Go on, now." The security officer nodded encouragement.

Hesitantly, the priest ducked under the railing and approached the pulpit. Still speaking, John finally noticed him but continued to the end of his current thought. Then he turned to Bertani and smiled, raising an eyebrow in inquiry.

Stepping away from the microphone, he said, "What is it, Alberto?"

"Holiness, I, ah," Bertani found himself tongue-tied, unable to speak.

"Talk to me, Alberto," the pope said with just a hint of impatience. "As you can see, my flock awaits." On the far side of the railing, the crowd shifted, a palpable unease growing as the front ranks watched this sidebar.

Swallowing, the priest found his voice and said, "Holiness, we have just been informed that Darwin is attacking Philosophia even as we speak. We may all already be dead men walking."

John searched Bertani's face for any hint of uncertainty or guile. There was none. Spotting the security officer, he waved her over and asked her to repeat what the priest had just told him. When she did, adding a few additional details, the pope asked about defenses.

She said, "Holy Father, we attempted to contact the *Lowell* as soon as Darwin was spotted but now have no way of knowing whether the message got through. We have never had planetary defenses on Philosophia, just the basic nanosystems that everyone in the belt has. Based on the Phobos experience, we expect the attacking wave of reducers to reach this level in approximately two hours."

"There is no way to stop them?"

"Unless the *Lowell* comes up with something, we can't stop this sort of attack. The only way out is via upload, but without somewhere off-planet to upload to, that's really not an option either. I'm sorry," she added with feeling.

The 271st pope closed his eyes and said, "I must tell these people something. The next few hours will be their last, and they deserve to die with dignity." He slowly returned to the pulpit, looking out at the faces turning to him expectantly as whispered conversations died away.

"My friends," he began.

~

On the bridge of the *Lowell*, Rooker was roaring in frustration. "Where the *hell* is Emerson? I need him in his gear now!"

"Sir," Lieutenant Denton said, "We've hailed him throughout the ship, but he's not responding. It's almost as if he's disappeared." She hesitated, then added, "I have some reason to think he may have been in Dr. Grosvenor's cabin a short while ago." Something in her voice caused Rooker to look at her, but there was no time to go into it.

"Then get down there and get him back here, Lieutenant. We'll deal with it later. And get Grosvenor up here as well, we may need him. I mean her." Two minutes later, Denton knocked on Grosvenor's door, which opened to reveal Mary's smiling face.

"Can I help you, Lieutenant?" she asked.

"Doctor, we've been informed that Philosophia is under attack and are returning at flank speed. The captain is requesting your presence on the bridge." Denton paused, then added, "We're also attempting to locate Officer Emerson, ma'am. Do you have any idea where he might be?"

"I'm afraid I can't help you with Mr. Emerson," Mary said, "but I'd be happy to join you on the bridge." Stepping through the door, she passed Denton and proceeded up the corridor. Before the door swung shut, the Lieutenant was able to see that no one else occupied the tiny cabin. She also saw the rumpled, unmade bed. Turning, she followed Grosvenor.

56

Once again, brain softeners were evident in Morrie Siegel's lab. Siegel, his grandfather Carl Herschberg, and Don Foster were sprawled on comfortable furniture discussing the nature of the human soul.

Foster was saying, "Well, who's to say the soul doesn't come along with consciousness when you do your scan, Morrie? I can't see how anyone could know the answer."

"The real problem," Siegel said slowly, "will come from those who will insist that the soul has a separate existence and has departed. They will think people like my grandfather are somehow less than human."

Turning to Herschberg, Foster said, "Well, how do you feel, Carl? You don't look like a zombie."

"I'm still having a little trouble grasping all that has happened," he replied. "You must understand, the change for me from the Dachau gas chamber to here was instantaneous. I felt no passage of time, certainly. So I'm still a bit muddled. But I can say that I feel like I'm all here; I don't feel as though part of me is missing or otherwise roaming out there like a, forgive me, lost soul."

Reaching for the Tanqueray, Foster said, "So, Morrie, how to ramp up? What could you do now, bring back maybe five or six people a day in your lab?"

"Perhaps a few more, but not many," the scientist said thoughtfully. "No, I have been thinking about this. There will eventually be millions of people wishing to resurrect loved ones, and millions more who don't, of course. The facilities to handle this would take up a small world and cost many billions. The whole enterprise is rather daunting, to say the least." The three men sat in quiet thought, a whisper of moving air the only sound.

"It also occurs to me," mused Siegel, "that if the project succeeds, it could bring many of the twenty-first century's resource and population issues back in a very big way."

Foster groaned and said, "Imagine what the Democrats could do with that! I moved out here to get away from all that nonsense."

As if not hearing him, Siegel continued, "But there are many thousands of asteroids, and hundreds of very substantial size that we haven't even begun to look at for settlement. On reflection, I think the environmental issues may be manageable."

After a moment, Herschberg cleared his throat and said, "Well, as it happens I may be able to help with the money." The other two looked at him curiously.

"Your grandmother inherited quite a bit of wealth from her own grandmother, a widow whose husband became quite prosperous during and after the Franco-Prussian war. Just before her death, she liquidated her holdings and placed all of her funds in trust with a Swiss bank. We never got around to paying any attention to the trust, and then the war came."

Foster broke in, "Carl, you can't believe that money's still there after, what, a hundred and sixty years?"

"I was able, thanks to the help of one of Morrie's young assistants, to check on that. The answer is yes, the money is still there and, as you might imagine, has grown rather considerably. What was a few million is now a significant number of billions. It is yours, Morrie. Use it to make this happen however you see fit. You're the only one who can."

Before Siegel could voice a reply, Foster said, "And it just so happens I have an asteroid you can use. Tell me how I can help."

Rising to fetch another bottle from the cupboard, Siegel said, "There is no adequate way to thank either of you for your generosity, except to actually do it. I guess we'd better make a list."

57

The last world of Paul-Pierre Henry was turning to ashes, and the imminence of death was having a strange effect on those within. Perhaps it was the pope's words, but the asteroid's miners, clerks, shopkeepers, and bureaucrats went about the business of their final hours calmly and deliberately. The unfortunates on or near the surface died quickly. Those in the deep caverns used their additional time to say farewells or, in some cases, to upload into the planetary Net to buy themselves additional time.

Once the Mass was over, security relocated the pontiff and his entourage to a nearby communications center used in normal times as a backup facility. John XXIV was quietly saying the rosary when all activity around him ceased as an image of the attacking vessel was captured on the main screen at the front of the room.

Someone at a nearby console muttered, "Lord, help us all."

Looking up, John gasped aloud. It had been many years since his summer vacation as a boy, but there was no mistaking the vision before him: Giacomo Borlone's Queen of Death had come calling.

An excited voice broke his concentration. "The *Lowell* is back! The *Lowell* is back!" A communications officer bent over his console in furious activity.

John watched as the image on the main screen dissolved and was replaced by Rooker's grim visage looking back. Then, his voice.

"Philosophia Central, this is Rooker aboard the *Lowell*. We are in-system and preparing to engage Darwin. Please give me your status." As he received the report on current conditions, Rooker's face became impassive, and he interrupted the communications officer.

"Listen carefully. We are targeting Darwin now. If we succeed, we will stand by for upload transfers as long as you're able to send them our way. We learned a hard lesson on Phobos and refitted all our ships with extra mass storage. If we fail, you're on your own." For a moment, Rooker was distracted by someone off-screen, then the face of Cardinal Josef Rauschman appeared.

"Convey this message to the Holy Father, please. I only have a moment to speak. You have important work to do, work which is not even close to being done. You must upload."

~

On the *Lowell's* bridge, Harry/Mary chose that moment to strike. While the cardinal spoke to Philosophia and Rooker gave Lieutenant Denton her final instructions, the Torcher focused on the weapons control officer, Rodriguez, raising a hand to point at his head. Before anyone could react, Rodriguez's head exploded. Brain, bone, and bright red blood splattered in all directions.

Appalled, Denton knew in a flash what was occurring. She and Rooker had their sidearms out and fired at the Torcher, who only smiled back at them and raised both arms to point at their heads. Just as they felt the beginning of intolerable heat, Cardinal Rauschman stepped in front of them, startling both them and their attacker. The Torcher redirected its concentration at Rauschman. Somehow unaffected, the cardinal stepped toward the creature, closing the distance quickly and reaching out to touch its brow. It shivered violently and collapsed.

Turning toward the two officers, who stood gaping at him, Rauschman said, "I will explain later, when there is time. This thing will not trouble you further. I suggest you proceed."

Recovering quickly, Rooker ordered two crewmen to remove the bodies. Picking up VR gear, he sat at the fire control console to prepare the attack. Denton, meanwhile, returned to the command chair to direct the *Lowell.*

"I don't know how in hell we're going to do this without Emerson's counterprogramming," Rooker muttered to no one in particular, "but we've got to try."

As the crewmen behind him cleaned up the mess, the lifeless Torcher began to deliquesce on the deck right before their eyes. It seemed to melt into a formless pile, drawing outraged exclamations from the crew. As Rooker, Denton, and Rauschman looked on apprehensively, the trillions of nanocomponents "read" the only instruction-set left to them and reassembled. Moments later, Emerson blinked up at them with what might charitably be called a confused expression.

The crewmen guffawed, Denton laughed out loud, and the cardinal colored. Emerson was quite naked, and it was clear what his most recent activity had included.

Rooker growled at the crewmen, "Get this idiot some pants. Emerson, put this VR gear on now; we're about to initiate."

~

On the far side of Philosophia, the Queen of Death looked down and was pleased. It was time to move on; Ceres beckoned, with its millions of not-so-immortals and millions more uploads polluting the system. After Ceres, Pallas, and after Pallas, Mars, then Luna and the orbiting colonies in near-space. And finally, when it had lost all its pathetic offspring, Mother Earth itself would be engulfed by the ultimate hell scenario.

Accelerating away from the doomed planet, the massive construct was unaware of the *Lowell* coming over the horizon or of the high-frequency directed carrier signal crossing its path. As they intersected, the signal inserted a long-string digital worm into one of the many interlinked matrices. The worm had two functions: replicate and erase. It performed both admirably, at least at first, spreading through the first of the many former sanctuaries, snuffing out electronic lives as it went. Within minutes, an entire sector of the construct had fallen silent forever. The seven million souls who remained noticed, and Darwin slowed to a stop, searching for the cause of its sudden misery and for a way to stop it.

On the bridge of the *Lowell,* Ayala Denton reported that the giant vessel had stopped and begun ranging with active sensors. Now in pants, Emerson, monitoring the worm's progress, reported that it had virtually ceased as Darwin put countermeasures into play.

"All right, Emerson, this is where you earn your lieutenant's bar," Rooker said. "Initiate secondary!"

Augmented by the shipboard AI, Emerson triggered a second directed burst he had designed to overcome the anticipated countermeasures. Worked out in advance with Rooker, the strategy was to keep coming at the mad vessel until it was scrubbed clean. Moments later, a second worm entered Darwin's lair. Using randomly variable sequencing, it quickly slipped past the electronic guardians and infected dozens more of the interior matrices. Insane as it was, Darwin's inhuman intelligence reacted almost immediately to the new invasion, bringing it to a halt after losing another three million components. Then it found the *Lowell.*

In the command chair, Denton stiffened. "Captain, Darwin has just launched. The PHASER will reach us in…seventy seconds."

"Hold steady, Lieutenant. We have to keep that beam right where it is. Emerson, where's number three?"

"Working on it, sir," replied Emerson, beads of sweat running into his eyes. Darwin was reacting more quickly than they had predicted, with the result that he had to reprogram on the fly. In his nearby observer's chair, Cardinal Rauschman's prayers turned from the lost electronic souls to the very much alive ones on the bridge. Emerson hit the "Execute" button.

As the third worm entered the construct, the ten-kilometer-high death's-head contorted in rage. This was not possible! How could such an insignificant, biological entity even presume to oppose the inevitable progress it represented? By the time it had destroyed the invader, another two million components were lost. The two million who were left were alternately outraged and terrified, with terror clearly ascendant. As Emerson labored to craft an effective fourth worm, the mad orb began to accelerate away in apparent hope of escape.

Licking her lips, Denton said, "Captain, we have twenty seconds until the PHASER strike."

"Son," Rooker said, placing his hand on Emerson's shoulder, "you've done more than anyone could have asked you to do. But I'm asking you one more time. And this one needs to work."

Nodding mutely, the young officer hit "Execute" for the last time.

"Ten seconds to PHASER impact," Denton said, and began counting down. Rauschman prayed. Rooker watched the main holo tank, which displayed a graphic of the construct and its components. Those that still functioned showed up red. As he looked, they began to turn gray one by one.

"Five, four, three..." Denton continued, only to have Cardinal Rauschman interrupt.

"Look at the screen!"

The primary display screen, used for those not linked in VR, showed the construct to be immobile and the death's-head to be missing. In the tank, all components showed gray.

"Impact!"

A cloud of mindless molecular Torchers engulfed the *Lowell*. Everyone on board held his or her breath, expecting instant disaster and death. Rooker didn't object when Denton took his hand and closed her eyes, nor when the cardinal stood and gave his blessing to those on the bridge. Instead, he looked steadily at Emerson who, after removing his headset, looked back with the beginnings of a smile tugging at his lips.

Putting an arm around Denton, Rooker said, "How much time, Walter?" It was the first time he had ever called Emerson by his first name, though no one seemed to notice.

Emerson glanced at a digital readout and said, "We're in the green by twelve seconds, sir."

Rauschman, sensing something new in the air, asked, "Captain? Would you care to enlighten us less fortunate souls as to why we are still here?" Rooker actually smiled before he replied.

"Of course, Eminence. Darwin's PHASER bursts are, or were, controlled via broadcast instructions. No Darwin means no instructions, and therefore no PHASER activity. We have indeed been hit, but the reducers on our hull are just so much space junk now. Our own maintenance 'bots will remove them in due course."

Applause and cheers resounded throughout the ship as the enormity of their accomplishment and survival set in. Emerson was high-fived and slapped on the back so many times he began to feel sore. Until, that is, Denton stood him up and gave him a resounding kiss, provoking even more cheers. Finally, Rooker reminded them their job was unfinished.

"Back to stations, people. We've got a rescue mission to accomplish." Sober once more, the crew returned to work, first sending a nuclear device into the heart of the husk that had once been home to over eleven million beings. As a flash lit up the sky behind them, the *Lowell* returned to Philosophia.

58

Despite Cardinal Rauschman's entreaty, John XXIV was not anxious to upload. The rather feeble objections emanating from Cardinal Llewellyn had nothing to do with his hesitation: he was genuinely unsure of the proper course. And then he got another look at Darwin. Long-ago memories of his uncle's farm had always been overlain by the Queen of Death. When he had looked at the queen on the comm center's main screen, John was suddenly at peace. *She must not prevail*, he thought, and allowed himself to be led to the subterranean medical facility whose personnel were feverishly processing those who wished to upload. He was still pondering Rauschman's final words when Father Bertani broke into his thoughts.

"Holiness, there is no more time."

"I know, Alberto. This feels like the right path, though only God knows for sure, and right now he's not talking." Removing the Ring of the Fisherman, John said, "Make sure Josef gets this, if by some miracle you survive." Turning to the attendant he continued, "Let's get on with it."

A white-suited technician led him to a comfortable chair while others worked at nearby consoles. A nurse handed him a flask containing billions of neurobots that would speed the process. He drank it without hesitation and sat down. After a few moments, he closed his eyes and appeared to sleep. Other technicians moved in with the accoutrements of uploading, and within minutes it was under way.

Elsewhere in the subterranean world, families sat holding hands, friends bid each other farewell, and lovers entwined in a final embrace. Pubs did a brisk business. The inexorable tide of molecular reducers was about to break through into the same level that held both the assembly hall and the backup (now primary) communications center. Still at his post, the duty officer was surprised to see the main screen light up again. An incoming call from the *Lowell* drew all eyes as Captain Charles Rooker's face appeared once more.

"Central, this is Rooker on the *Lowell.* Glad to see you're still with us. I'm calling to report that we have destroyed the intruder; please update your status."

Finding his voice with some difficulty, the duty officer responded, "That is welcome news, Captain. We are showing planetwide destruction of approximately 40 percent, population attrition of 36 percent, and expect the attack to reach our current level within, ah, six minutes." Before he could continue, a subordinate's excited voice interrupted.

"Sir, instruments read that the attacking wave has stopped moving. I repeat, the attack seems to be over!" The duty officer slumped in his seat as cheers broke out. *I've got to find a new line of work,* he thought.

A new voice came through from the *Lowell.*

"Central, this is Cardinal Josef Rauschman. Can you tell me, please, the status of the Holy Father? I would like to speak with him as soon as possible."

Forgetting he had a prince of the Church on the line, the duty officer exclaimed "Jesuschrist!" and picked up a handset. Two minutes later, the ashen-faced officer informed the *Lowell* that the 271st pontiff had, in fact, already been uploaded.

~

About to enter a final approach pattern to Philosophia, the papal ferry's AI was instructed by the *Lowell* to put the ship into orbit while things were sorted out. Carolyn, Sarah, and Jack were distracted tending to Adler. When Darwin had succumbed to the *Lowell's* attack, the big man had gone into spasms that threatened to break bones and splinter furnishings. He had since been quiescent but had not regained consciousness. Looking at Sarah's stricken face, Jack fervently hoped the man would wake up soon.

Three very long hours later, a groan escaped Adler's slightly parted lips. He rolled to one side, then sat up with help from Carolyn and Sarah. He drank the water Carolyn offered.

"It's gone," he said, shaking his head. "I don't know how or why, but it's just plain not there anymore." With an effort, he got to his feet and looked around, frowning before he remembered where they were.

Then his face cleared, and he picked up Sarah in an intense embrace.

"Well," Jack said, "I guess we're going to be all right."

Carolyn smiled, kissed his cheek, and said, "Better tend to the ship, sailor. Someone's knocking on the door." The other three looked at the screens, which indicated an incoming call. When Adler brought it up, they were all surprised to see Cardinal Rauschman's face looking back. He and Sarah were introduced, then he got down to business.

"You should expect two transfers over the next few hours, one from the *Lowell* returning me, and one from the surface bringing Father Bertani and most of the others. There will be an electronic transfer from the surface as well. I will tell you more about it when I arrive."

Rauschman's grim demeanor unsettled her, and Carolyn said, "Eminence, we look forward to your return. Will the Holy Father be joining us as well?"

"In a manner of speaking. I will bring you up to date in, oh, about ninety minutes." With that, he ended the call, and the four travelers looked at each other in confusion. And in Carolyn's case, a growing sense of dread.

59

Neuroscanning had advanced to a sophisticated, mature science by the early twenty-second century. Upon awakening, John XXIV found himself seated once more in a comfortable chair, only this time surrounded by digital avatars designed to ease the transition to electronic life. A young woman asked him how he felt.

"Why, I feel the same, I suppose," he said slowly. "I certainly didn't expect this sort of reception, though. Does everyone who goes through uploading have a similar experience?"

"We try to make it as seamless as possible, Holiness. The underlying principle is to introduce you gradually to the digital electronic world by starting with something you're familiar with. When you're ready, you go through that door and begin your new life. That's assuming Darwin is stopped, of course." As John pondered her words, all activity seemed to stop momentarily, then resume. She looked at him with an unreadable expression on her face.

"Holiness, we have just been informed that Darwin has, in fact, been destroyed by Captain Rooker and his crew. The attack on Philosophia has ended."

Thinking about the irony in life, John XXIV rose and said, "I think I'd like to see what's on the other side of that door, miss." The avatar led him to the portal, then turned.

"This is not like anything else. You will find that you can move, change your point of view, communicate with others, even merge with others all in less time than it used to take to blink your eyes. It is orderly, as you would expect, but there is chaos as well. Those who do well seem to find a way to ignore the chaos, or at least to ignore those who become lost in it. Listen, for I imagine there will be those who wish to speak with you."

He thanked her and stepped through. The door closed.

60

Adler wasn't exactly a prisoner. His central, albeit unwilling, role in the tracking of Darwin had led directly to its destruction, so the authorities were inclined to forgive and forget. Upon his return, the ferry captain had banished him from the bridge, but otherwise the crew and passengers treated him quite well—as a minor celebrity, even. He began to hope there would be a life for him and Sarah after all.

They stood at the rear of the salon, where Cardinal Rauschman had called everyone to a meeting. The entire complement of crew and passengers had assembled in the rather cramped space as he strode to the front of the room.

"My friends, during the attack on Philosophia it seemed clear to those on the ground that they were about to be overwhelmed. For reasons I won't bother reviewing now, the Holy Father was uploaded." Several in the crowd gasped. Sarah's fingers dug into Adler's arm. Standing nearby, Carolyn buried her face in Jack's chest. The cardinal continued.

"We are going to remain in orbit until he can be transferred to our own media. This should not take long, but at the moment those on the surface are unable to locate him. I'm sure this is just temporary; please be patient." He looked everyone in the eye before bowing his head and saying, "Now if you would, please pray with me."

~

Alberto Bertani was pacing like a man possessed. The medical center was on high alert as its technicians made repeated attempts to contact the pontiff, and Bertani allowed himself the luxury of cursing to relieve some of the stress he felt. He would perhaps have been less agitated were it not for the smug look on Cardinal Llewellyn's face. He knew it meant trouble. Llewellyn *always* meant trouble.

Several hours later, a young, white-garbed worker looked up from his VR console and shouted, "I've got him!" Bertani rushed over and donned the headset indicated by the technician. The sights and sounds of the medical center faded away, replaced by what appeared to be a small, comfortable room occupied only by John XXIV, who smiled at him.

"Alberto, I'm glad to see you. I am having the most extraordinary experience and want to tell you about my new mission."

The young priest had difficult speaking, overcome as he was by the loss of his mentor's physical presence and the tragedy that created for his beloved Church. Then the pope's words sunk in.

"New mission, Holiness?"

"Indeed, my young friend. Do you realize how many millions of people are living electronic lives without benefit of spiritual counsel, let alone the sacraments? I have spent the last hours getting to know some of these people. They hunger for the Word, Alberto. I think I understand Darwin now and how its hubris could have grown in a moral vacuum to lead it to the terrible course it embarked upon. We must never let that happen again.

"Let's talk about the future."

As the remainder of the papal entourage boarded the ferry hours later, Rauschman noted the disgruntled look on Llewellyn's face and felt the beginnings of hope. He accepted the cushioned package from Father Bertani and took it to the bridge, where the communications officer transferred its digital contents to the ship's own storage. Ten minutes later, he and the pope were making plans. An hour later, the ferry left orbit bound for the Inner System.

61

Angela Ford didn't really miss the Hog and Hen. Her duties as security chief had made the occasional visit necessary, but in general it had been a fairly tame taproom. No, what she missed was the simpler time the pub represented in her memory, a time when TPUD housed a mere four hundred souls. A time when visitors were few and quite far between. A time when there was not incessant, around-the-clock construction going on somewhere within the asteroid. And mostly, a time when she got a solid six hours' sleep almost every night. That time, she knew, was gone forever. And TPUD even had a new name. Uncle Don Foster, damn him, had come up with it one day after a mere three brain softeners: Resurrection City. Once she understood what was in the offing, Angela had to admit that it made sense.

As the entry doors opened in the arrivals lounge, she stepped forward to welcome the newest guests, only to stop and stare in disbelief at the first one through. Captain Jack Anders grinned as he gave her a hug.

"Angie, I can't tell you how good it is to see you again! Feels like we've been traveling for months. Well, we have, actually. Meet my friends.

"Carolyn West, whom you may remember from the pope's visit; Sarah Chase, recently in from Pallas, and the big fella's Quentin Adler." Angela collected herself and shook hands in turn with the two women and very large man. Before she had a chance to get into her welcome speech, Foster came rushing in.

"Jack, boy, it's about time you got back! I send you over to Zion for a couple of days, and you're gone for three months? And Carolyn, I'm glad you decided to come back after all. I hope Jack's treating you better than he's treating me." He went on, renewing his acquaintance with Quentin before turning to Sarah.

"And you, young lady, you're the most important person here." As Sarah beamed at him, he said, "Welcome to Resurrection City, formerly known as The Planet Uncle Don. We have a terrific little pub that's in serious need of attention."

Offering her his arm, he said to the others, "Follow me." A bemused Angela Ford watched as Don and his entourage proceeded down the main corridor.

~

In the spotless new lab adjacent to the nearly complete resuscitation chambers, Morrie Siegel drummed his fingers on his desktop. He'd been obsessed for weeks with the facility's construction. Now that the end was in sight, his thoughts had returned to the relatively abstract discipline of quantum mechanics.

He had shut himself in the lab two days ago, running molecular simulations with the resident AI around the clock in an effort to model ionized hydrogen atoms as computers. Well, as databanks, anyway. He had a vague idea, and he was close to making it work.

For many long years, he had wanted justice. Now he would settle for vengeance.

62

For the first time in its twenty-one-hundred-year history, the Church had called a conclave while the issue of the pope's death was in dispute. Certainly there had been other times, other controversies. Benedict IX occupied the Throne of Peter three different times in the eleventh century, and antipopes had been common throughout the middle ages. But nothing compared to the uproar currently sweeping through Rome.

Word of John XXIV's upload had reached Earth, and at the behest of the more traditional members of the Curia, the Cardinal Camerlengo had notified the College of Cardinals that a conclave would be held. There was no body to witness over, no ring to cut, no shield to destroy, but no matter. Since there was no walking, talking pope either, an election was required. Upon his return to Earth, Cardinal Llewellyn had been among the more outspoken advocates of this course, whispering daily in the ears of his brethren. Curiously, the formidable Cardinal Rauschman was silent.

As the final stanza of the *Veni Creator Spiritus* filled the vault of the Sistine Chapel, Rauschman glanced behind the altar one more time to appreciate Michelangelo's astonishing depiction of the Last Judgment. He wondered for perhaps the hundredth or thousandth time, *are we the Damned or the Elect?* As the cardinals took the oath one by one, he thought, *perhaps what we do today will have something to do with the answer.*

The few servants and functionaries who were still present were ordered out and the doors were locked. Shifting in their seats, clearing their throats, glancing furtively at their neighbors, it seemed that no one quite knew what to do.

Until the austere Cardinal Odinga stood. The Kenyan had become secretary of state ten years earlier and had performed the number-two position's duties with quiet dignity ever since. Not, perhaps, universally loved, he was respected by everyone present. The press treated him as one of the foremost *papabile*, quite possibly in line to become the first modern pope of African descent.

"Eminences. I am deeply troubled by the events that have brought us together. I would prefer to be almost anywhere else, to tell you the truth. The Holy Father and I were close for many years, and I feel the impact of his absence most acutely both in my daily rituals and in those of the greater Church we serve."

Looking now at Rauschman, he continued, "I know you all join me in this and would ask my brothers who accompanied John to tell us what they know." He sat back down to renewed murmurings.

Llewellyn rose next and gave a reasonably accurate account of the circumstances surrounding the upload. His portrayal of the attack on Philosophia was perhaps a bit exaggerated, but except for the fleeting smile that crossed Rauschman's face, no one seemed to realize it. Father Bertani had been asked to join this session of the conclave and gave his own testimony next. The young priest was clearly awed by the gathering and the venue, but there was no mistaking the sincerity in his voice.

"The Holy Father placed himself in God's hands," he said respectfully. "We all expected to die shortly, and uploading was the only way he might continue to serve the Church." He looked stricken as he said, "I would gladly have accompanied him, but he gave me a task to perform if I survived." Bertani rose and approached the front rank of cardinals, where Rauschman was seated.

Handing him the Ring of the Fisherman, he said, "Eminence, he asked that I hold his ring and give it to you if we survived. He said that you would know what to do."

As he returned to his seat, the quiet murmuring grew in volume and agitation. It seemed that each member of the College of Cardinals had something to say to his immediate neighbors and chose that moment to do so. The Cardinal Camerlengo stood to restore order but held his tongue after a glance at Rauschman. Best to let them jabber then. But when four minutes had passed with no noticeable diminution in volume, Rauschman rose to his feet. The effect was immediate.

In the ensuing silence, he said simply, "Bide a moment, if you will." He then beckoned to Bertani, and the two men moved to the foot of the chapel where a table held a variety of accessory devices. One of these was a small but powerful computer. Another, judging by the speakers, had something to do with sound reproduction. After flipping some switches and briefly studying a screen, the men returned to their seats, where Rauschman remained standing.

"My friends, thank you for indulging me. All will be clear shortly." He paused and looked at the assembled faces, smiled, and said, "It's probably fair to say that I was not known to be one of the Holy Father's biggest fans." The unexpected levity confused many of his brethren but amused even more, who visibly relaxed. Rauschman went on.

"That reputation was perhaps deserved, but it obscured the fact that I felt, as most of you did, that our friend from Venice was this Church's best hope for the future. You all would have been proud of him on the space journey. He was well on his way to spreading God's Word throughout the belt. He more than held his own on Eros. And he understood, as none of his predecessors have, how the changes sweeping through our culture required, no, *demanded* a moral context."

Odinga quietly said, "You'll get no argument on this from anyone here, Josef. But where are you going? Not to put too fine a point on it, but where are *we* going?"

"The future is no more clear to me today than it was yesterday," said Rauschman. "I would like to address your question to the one whose actions have brought us here today."

Seeing mostly puzzled faces, he turned to the table at the foot of the assembly and said, "Holiness? Will you speak?"

After a moment, a warm, familiar voice began, "Eminences, I am glad to be with you today. Please pray with me."

63

Dachau, Third Reich, 1945—Dr. Sigmund Rascher was not pleased. He had finally come to a grudging acceptance of his arrest and imprisonment; after all, he and his wife had technically broken the law when they took in the orphans. Karoline had always wanted more children, and there certainly were plenty to spare around the camps. He hadn't expected Himmler's fury upon learning of the "adoptions" though. That was a miscalculation on his part, one he would not make again, assuming he ever got out of this godforsaken place.

No, the arrest was justified. What was ruining his normally placid disposition this morning was his recent relocation back to Dachau. For multiple reasons, this was not a healthy place for him to be, although he had to admit that the accommodations could have been worse. Upon his arrival, he had been taken directly to the Lagerarrest and locked in cell seventy-three. He was allowed outside every day, fed well, and treated respectfully by the guards, many of whom had followed his orders unquestioningly not long ago. But the prisoners! It was clear every time he went outside that the subhumans knew who he was, and he knew that, given the chance, they would kill him without hesitation. Animals. Hopefully, the Americans would get here first.

His musings were interrupted by footsteps outside his door. Someone was coming his way down the long, narrow corridor. Someone with purpose.

After a moment the door swung open, and in walked Hauptscharführer Theodor Bongartz. He bowed slightly, wearing a thin smile that did not reach beyond his lips. Behind him, a large, gun-toting guard filled the hall.

"Herr Doktor, I am pleased to tell you that we have received new orders from Reichsführer Himmler concerning yourself. You are to gather your possessions and return to Berlin at once."

This did not sound like good news to Rascher, not good at all. Berlin was a city under siege. Every thinking person, including Himmler, knew that in a matter of days or weeks the Third Reich would be history. What was the point of returning to the capital now? He knew that Bongartz would be useless: as in all matters, the SS officer would follow Himmler's orders to the letter. Pathetic, really.

Attempting a smile, Rascher stood and said, "Indeed, Hauptscharführer, that is most welcome. A moment, if you will. I have only a few things to bring."

Rascher turned in the cramped cell to retrieve the few books and articles of clothing he had been allowed to keep. He was forced to lean over the tiny writing desk, and when he straightened up he felt the press of cold steel against the base of his skull.

"Doktor, you may in fact be returned to Berlin; that is not for me to decide. If you are, it will be in a coffin. The Reichsführer has ordered your death."

"Bongartz," he said through a suddenly dry mouth, "I have money. You're going to need it in the days to come. Trade me for my life."

He turned around and looked into the barrel of the SS man's sidearm. There was no interest, no pity on the face before him, and he grabbed the gun with both hands to force it upward. A shot rang out, burying itself in the ceiling. Behind the struggling men, the guard made a futile attempt to enter the room before a second bullet plowed through his left eye and destroyed his brain, dropping him to the floor. Enraged, the SS officer freed a hand and grabbed Rascher's testicles in a squeeze.

The Nazi doctor howled in agony and fell to his knees, releasing the gun. Before he could recover, he felt an incredible blow explode against the back of his head. Then, he felt nothing at all.

Three days later, the Third Battalion of the 157th U.S. Infantry Regiment entered the camp. Rascher's corpse was one among thousands.

~

Morrie Siegel sat back and rubbed his ashen face. He had experienced unbearable tension as he had narrowed the remote scan until the focus was quite clearly on Rascher at his penultimate moment. Looking at the electronic telltales, he knew the scan had been successful. It was time for step two.

64

Located close to the inner rim of the Orion Arm, the Sun orbits the Milky Way's galactic center once every 225–250 million years. A G2V star, it fuses hydrogen into helium every second of every day, just as it has for the last four or five billion years. Scientists believe it will keep doing so for another four or five billion.

At its surface, the Sun reaches temperatures of over 9,400 degrees Fahrenheit—real heat by anyone's standards. Deep within its core, way down where the fusion takes place and pressures are immense, the conditions are nearly unimaginable. Ten times as dense as lead, the core is kept gaseous by the nuclear heat as hydrogen nuclei are continuously fused into helium—eighty-nine undecillion of them (that's "89" followed by thirty-six zeroes) every second. Temperatures reach twenty-seven *million* degrees.

Awareness returned slowly to Sigmund Rascher. When he had recovered sufficiently, he was amazed to find that he still existed after all; the fool Bongartz must have shot him in the head. His surprise quickly gave way to confusion, however. He had no visual clues as to his whereabouts and no other hints as to his condition. He had an impression of vast, roiling space punctuated by iridescent clouds, then of incredible heat and pressure. As the heat drew his attention more firmly, his warped but analytic mind was astonished to realize that he was somehow floating in a sea of fire, a sea that had no up or down and no surface. He realized he could "move" after a fashion by willing his point of view to change. He did so, entering one of the passing clouds and finding himself swept by an irresistible current that disoriented and dimmed his perceptions almost to extinction as it seemed to shred him into an infinity of specks. After a very long time, he regained enough awareness to find himself back in the sea, or whatever it was. Though he didn't experience the heat and pressure directly, their ubiquitous presence began to prey on him, and he attempted another cloud, again nearly losing himself. And again. And many agains, without number, until he finally realized that the Sunday school stories he had dismissed as fairy tales had, in fact, been true.

Hell was real.

65

For the first time in memory, perhaps in history, a papal conclave had ended without the selection of a new pope. The faithful waiting in St. Peter's Square had been confused, then overjoyed, when the Cardinal Deacon had appeared on the basilica's main balcony to announce that the "new" pope was in fact the "old" pope, John XXIV. He would remain in office, an electronic but completely human presence who would continue to be ably assisted by Cardinal Odinga, Cardinal Rauschman, and the newly minted Monsignor Bertani. A million voices roared their approval.

Somewhat later, Rauschman entered his quarters in the Vatican, thinking back to the final hours of the conclave. It had not been easy. John's dramatic voice had calmed many, but not all fears, and when Thomas Llewellyn complained about the extension of John's lifespan perhaps indefinitely, he had seen the "hmmm" look on many faces. The pope's continued presence as an upload would have far-reaching ramifications for many of the orthodox views currently predominant in Church teaching. Musing, he turned at the sound of a knock.

"Enter."

Resplendent in his new, red-trimmed black cassock, Alberto Bertani looked contrite as he opened the door.

"My apologies, Eminence, but the Holy Father wishes to converse with you and Cardinal Odinga. It will only take a few minutes of your time."

"Don't be silly, Alberto, that's what we're here for." Noticing the tall African behind the priest, Rauschman said, "Please come in and make yourselves comfortable."

"Thank you, Josef," said Odinga as Bertani stepped aside to allow him to enter first. As the men took seats, Bertani placed a duffel on the floor and withdrew a small computer, which he set on a table and powered up. To the cardinals' surprise, he then withdrew a bottle of brandy and three glasses, which he also set on the table. Looking askance, Rauschman raised an eyebrow.

Nonplussed, Bertani stammered, "Your pardon, Eminences. I am merely following his Holiness's wishes in this matter. I do not know the purpose."

"Well," said Odinga with a smile, "Our friend from Venice is just full of surprises."

The computer came alive, and moments later John XXIV joined the conversation.

"Thank you for giving me your time, Eminences. It won't take long, but there are two matters that must be attended to immediately. First is the condition of the Vatican's electronic infrastructure, which, as you know, is nearly a century old. Now that I, ah, *live* in it, I understand just how far behind the times we are and how much the lack of current technology hinders our ability to interact with the far-flung members of our flock. This must change, quickly."

"Holiness," said Odinga, "I'm sure you know I agree with you. With your authority the three of us can and will make this happen. But surely you didn't assemble us just to deal with technology?"

"You are quite correct, my friend, there is another matter. I will leave it to Josef and Alberto to brief you concerning developments on the asteroid Zion, where events have transpired that will affect us all. Without going into detail, I wish to say only that matters there require our urgent attention."

Bertani leaned forward in his seat and said, "Holiness, do you mean to say that we're going back?"

"I'm afraid so, Alberto. As soon as possible."

Exhaling slowly, Rauschman looked at Odinga, then reached for the brandy.

66

Shaking his head in amusement, Captain Jack poured another round of drinks. Since Sarah had taken over, the Hog and Hen had recovered nicely, expanding to the point where it was now almost a required stop for any visitor within sixty degrees of the belt. But some things hadn't changed. Down at the end of the bar, Don Foster and Morrie Siegel were arguing about something exotic. Morrie was taking one of his infrequent breaks from the resurrection operation. Jack thought the scientist looked gaunt, almost haunted, yet here he was in the midst of the greatest scientific achievement in human history. Go figure.

Carolyn walked by and smiled at him. She had become the best part of Jack's life, and he had actually begun to hope for a future together. She had gone to work for Morrie and had quickly become the resurrection operation's chief coordinator, handling the logistics as well as the growing volume of requests and research. No longer averse to electronic life, she interacted constantly with the AIs and uploads who performed most of the work. *Best of all*, he thought to himself, *she actually seems to like me.*

A group of construction workers came in trailing a very thirsty-looking Quentin Adler. They settled in at a corner table, then hooted appreciatively as

Sarah came over and planted an affectionate kiss on his dusty lips. Evading his grasp, she took their order and came behind the bar to help Jack fill it. Adler had been working almost nonstop on expansion projects, first at the Hog and Hen, then over at the labs and new transitional accommodations. All the major hotel chains had come calling and were now fixtures on the tiny world. "Returnees" were treated very well indeed.

Earlier in the day, Sarah and Quentin had hosted a small lunch in the private dining room. Jack, Carolyn, Don, and Morrie had been joined by the visiting Cardinal Rauschman and Captain Rooker, accompanied by Lieutenants Denton and Emerson. As the wine had flowed, recent events began to make sense.

"What was the story on Harry Grosvenor?" Carolyn wanted to know.

Morrie said, "We learned that there really was such a person, at least originally. It seems likely that he was erased by Darwin, who then used his template to create an agent."

"But why the sex change?"

"That," said Rooker, "was just a red herring to mask what was really going on. It came way too close to working." With those words he turned to the cardinal, an inquiring look on his face.

"Eminence? Would you care to enlighten the rest of us?" Rauschman looked uncomfortable for a moment, then shrugged and held up a palm facing outward.

"When I was young and more foolish than I hope I am these days, I sought every macroenhancement I could find. One of these was a modification of the old-fashioned electric cattle prod. Look closely at the tip of my finger." As the others leaned in he continued, "You'll see an embedded metallic pinhead. All I did was blank the creature's operating instruction-sets with a jolt of electricity."

"Thus ending the crisis and paving the way for Emerson's return," said Denton.

"Indeed," Rauschman said before changing the subject. "Morrie, your work is obviously going well, yet you seem quite distracted."

Putting down his drink, the scientist shook his head and said, "There are certain problems we may never overcome. Foremost among them is the spatial-temporal focus; we simply can't resurrect anyone we can't precisely locate in time and space. That, it turns out, includes most of the 120 billion or so people who have ever lived."

As the group considered that sobering news, the new Monsignor Bertani entered and whispered into Rauschman's ear. The cardinal stood.

"If you'll excuse me, Alberto has news that requires my attention. Miss Chase, many thanks for a delicious meal. Morrie, do you have a few minutes?" The three men departed as the meal drew to a close.

The sight of celebrities no longer excited Jack as it once had. Truth be told, they were a dime a dozen in Resurrection City as they made their way off-planet. He was just too busy to wonder where they were going, though every now and then one chose to hang around for a while, usually at the Hog and Hen. At one table General George Armstrong Custer was deep in conversation with Crazy Horse, while a third man someone claimed was Genghis Khan looked on. Nearby, Humphrey Bogart and Lauren Bacall were playing cards with Katharine Hepburn and Spencer Tracy.

Many of the less-famous also passed through, though seldom stayed long. Returnees who had once been concentration camp inmates seemed to have little interest in the pub or night life. Jack thought he understood but knew he really had no idea.

He did wonder briefly about Bertani's interruption at lunch; he was curious but hadn't had time to investigate. Now, with day slipping into evening, it was almost time for the nightly entertainment to begin. One of Quentin's first projects had been the addition of a second dining area complete with a stage, and the large room was rapidly filling. Sarah had promised something special.

As Jack struggled to keep up with the orders, a commotion drew his attention to the door. A small group led by Monsignor Bertani was coming in, and he caught a glimpse of the imposing Cardinal Rauschman before a waitress demanded his attention. Engaged in pouring the drinks, he was startled to hear a familiar voice.

"Captain, I'm very happy to see you again. I see you're busy, so I won't trouble you further, just wanted to say hello." Glancing up, his jaw dropped as he looked into the smiling face of John XXIV, 271st (and last) bishop of Rome. The white pontifical robes were almost iridescent on the man as he moved through the crowded taproom and took a seat at the rear of the new dining room. *Of course,* thought Jack. *Come see Morrie, get the Uncle Don treatment.*

As the lights dimmed in the new dining room, Sarah took the stage and welcomed everyone, paying special attention to her famous guests. The room finally quieted.

"Ladies and gentlemen, we're very pleased this evening to bring you music that hasn't been heard live in many, many years. Sit back and enjoy the show." The curtain began to rise on a band that launched into a bluesy, honky-tonk rendition of an old rock and roll classic. Sitting at the pope's table, Charles Rooker grunted. The guitar sure sounded like… Nah, it couldn't be, could it? The stage lights came up, revealing Jimi Hendrix on lead guitar and Ray Charles on piano. Rooker laughed out loud when a gyrating vocalist entered from stage-right and began to sing:

You ain't nothin' but a hound dog, cryin' all the time.

You ain't nothin' but a hound dog, cryin' all the time.

You ain't never caught a rabbit and you ain't no friend of mine.

Two hundred thirty million miles away, the molecular pattern formerly known as Sigmund Rascher was joined by one, then another former luminary of the Third Reich. Together, they writhed in the deepest pit of hell.

ACKNOWLEDGEMENTS

I now have a slightly better sense of how one gets from an idea to a book, and for that knowledge I thank everyone who has helped me:

My kids, Rachel, John, and Charlie, who taught me how to tell stories.

My wife Loron, who not only put up with all the nonsense but actually supported me throughout.

My brother Charlie, ace beta-tester and constructive critic.

My partner Stephanie, who encouraged me and who may eventually give me a moment's peace when the book is published (but probably not).

Tara Weaver, who suffered through an early edit and gave me much constructive feedback.

Gail Cato, who suffered through a later edit and turns out to have great taste in music.

Jessica Smith, the copy editor who appreciates good words.

The folks at BookSurge who patiently got me through this: Kelly, Lindsay, David, Karen, Lauren, Blair, Emma, Julian, and any others I've neglected to mention.

AFTERWORD

Half of the proceeds from the sales of this book will go to a charity I helped found almost ten years ago, the Choroideremia Research Foundation, Inc. Choroideremia is a rare disorder of the eye that steals one's vision in small increments over many years. It's inherited on the X chromosome, meaning that women are "carriers" and men are, well, blinded eventually. My brother Matt and I are affected; our mother and my daughter are carriers.

Science can do amazing things when harnessed for good, but scientists have to pay the bills just like the rest of us. It is my fervent hope that this book, and those to follow, will help them do just that in the quest for a better, sighted world.

The Foundation's website is www.choroideremia.org.

Made in the USA